Young Lions

A Child of Their Own

Mrs Darling kept thinking about the Serious Collector and feeling more than a little bit frightened. Because, as you already know, the worst thing that can happen to a doll is never to be played with and forgotten for weeks and months and years at a time. Then the doll often becomes very lonely. Dolls that have been neglected for too long or that have never been played with at all lose themselves completely. If you go to a museum, look at the antique dolls – some are lively and look right back at you, but others, you may notice, are only the shell of a doll – they don't really seem to be there. These are the poor dolls who were never loved. They have become knick-knacks and are lost forever.

Mary had told Mrs Darling all about getting lost. This is what Mrs Darling was afraid might happen if the American Lady was a Serious Collector and just put them on a shelf. Of course all of the Darlings were curious about her . . .

Other Young Lions Storybooks

Justine Rendal

A Child
of Their Own

Illustrated by Sian Bailey

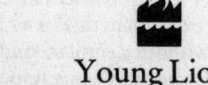

Young Lions
An Imprint of HarperCollinsPublishers

First published 1990 by
William Collins Sons & Co Ltd
First published in Young Lions 1992

Young Lions is an imprint of
the Children's Division, part of
HarperCollins Publishers Ltd,
77–85 Fulham Palace Road, Hammersmith,
London W6 8JB

Text copyright © Justine Rendal 1990
Illustrations copyright © Sian Bailey 1990

The author asserts the moral right to be
identified as the author of this work.

ISBN 0 00 674296-3

Printed and bound in Great Britain by
HarperCollins Manufacturing, Glasgow

To Randy, when she was four,
and to Brendan,
the original Johnsley.

Contents

1
The Beginning of It

They lived at first in a glass case in a London toy shop, just beside the register. Of course, when I say "lived", I don't mean it as we do for people, for dolls don't have the exact kind of life that we do. They don't breathe or eat or sleep as we do. But they do have a life, just the same.

The Darlings (for that is what everyone called them, and so they thought it was their proper name) were cushioned on white tissue paper in a long row. Mr Darling was dressed in a blazer and waistcoat as an English gentleman. His noble head was topped by fair and wavy hair and he was just a little bit over six inches tall.

"Just a hair over," he would say, "but that is quite something for a doll."

"Indeed, you are far taller than I," said Mrs Darling. She had dark auburn hair, swept up in loops and curls that made a beautiful swirl at the back. Her dress was real silk and swirled at the back too. A soft shade of pink, it was trimmed with the most delicate real lace. Nicest of all, she had a kind and pretty face. She also had good grammar, and she knew what a doll needed to feel good.

"I always think it particularly nice that you are over six inches tall," she would say to Mr Darling.

"Well, just a hair over," replied Mr Darling modestly.

On either side of them were the children: Johnsley, who was six and as fair as his father, Enid who was seven, "going on eight," she'd say, and Eugenia, the baby who was dressed in a heavenly blue satin coat and a lace-trimmed bonnet. Her painted smile was broad and mischievous. Lastly there was Emma, who was much older than you, but not quite grown up yet. She liked, however, to act grown up. In fact she was more than a little bit bossy, as some big sisters are.

Beside Emma was a brother and sister doll set, and they are quite important in this story. There were a lot of other dolls in the glass case too but it was the Darlings who drew the most attention and who were by far the most expensive.

"They are made of finest porcelain and handpainted," the Shopkeeper would say, when people bent over the case. "And their clothes are all exquisitely done by hand. They are *very* fine."

This made the Darlings feel very proud. But almost as often, the Shopkeeper would add: "They aren't meant as playthings really. They are too delicate. They are more for the Serious Collector."

These two words always upset Mrs Darling, though she tried not to show it. "Serious Collector" did not sound like someone who would play with them. For dolls cannot truly come alive, cannot have adventures or birthday parties or a cosy evening meal round the dining table unless a child plays with them.

"I hope we aren't bought by a Serious Collector," thought Mrs Darling. "We must not be." And her lovely porcelain face would look frightened.

The brother and sister doll set beside the Darlings in the glass case were not made of fine porcelain. "Only cheap china. Mass-produced," the Shopkeeper would remark. And somehow that made them sound unimportant. But despite that, the girl doll's chin was firm and her dark grey eyes were direct and full of determination. Her brush of auburn hair was long and wild. She was about the same age as Enid Darling or perhaps a bit older. Her name was Amanda Miranda. Her brother's name was Revely and she loved him very much. Amanda Miranda wished more than anything that she was a Darling. Secretly sometimes she would whisper "Amanda Miranda Darling" to herself. But she was far too shy to tell anyone her secret wish, not even Revely.

She and Revely were dressed in lumpy grey velvet sailor suits. "Glued, not sewn," explained the Shopkeeper, who was honest, if unkind. It was true their clothes looked shabby and had none of the fine-sewn details that the Darling's splendid costumes had. Yet, for some reason, despite the lumpy clothes, most people looking into the case believed Amanda Miranda and Revely were part of the family. Maybe it was because they were placed right beside the Darlings, or because their hair was auburn, as Mrs Darling's was, or because their clothes were also Edwardian, even if they were glued and not sewn. Or maybe it was because Amanda Miranda wished so much to be a Darling. Whatever the reason, it happened often. And Mr and Mrs Darling didn't seem to mind. In fact, sometimes Amanda Miranda dared to hope that they liked it.

"You are becoming quite a member of the family," said Mr Darling one afternoon as all of them were being admired by some shoppers. And Amanda Miranda felt very warm inside.

"Perhaps it *is* possible," she thought.

"Well they're not," said Emma, the older sister. "They are not nearly as fine as us." None of the shoppers had singled her out for admiration that day and she was rather hurt and angry.

"As *we*. And I think Amanda Miranda and Revely are quite as good as we are," said Mrs Darling, correcting both Emma's grammar and her manners.

"But they are only mass-produced," objected Emma; although she didn't know exactly what that meant, she knew it wasn't particularly good.

"No one is mass-produced," said Mrs Darling. "Each of us is made just once, fast or slow, by hand or machine. And Amanda Miranda has *such* fine eyes."

"Well, the Shopkeeper said she was," insisted Emma, who was more than a little stubborn.

"The Shopkeeper doesn't know everything," responded Mrs Darling, and thought of the Serious

Collector. She shuddered, and once again hoped the Shopkeeper was wrong about who would buy them. She wished so much for a kind child who would love them and play with them for a long, long time.

"Well, anyway, Amanda Miranda and Revely were not made as part of the family," persisted Emma.

"Families are not made, they become," said Mrs Darling. "In all families, members are added one by one, some as babies, some in other ways. And sometimes families lose members too. Isn't it lovely that we can all be together now?" Mrs Darling had another terrible fear, even worse than her fear of being bought by the Serious Collector. It was so bad she would not even think of it most of the time. But Emma had reminded her. For a doll family can be separated, sold to different people or even given away. And dolls can be lost, or shattered beyond repair. Mrs Darling could not bear even to think of such a thing.

Emma was not really mean, she was only a little jealous. Like many dolls (and some people, too) she was sometimes afraid that if others got love, the supply would run out. She did not realize that love doesn't work that way, and I hope you know it.

So the Darlings, and Amanda Miranda and Revely, too, lived for the time being in the shop's place of honour in the glass case. This might seem like quite a dull life to you, tucked up in a case all day and night, but while it was far from perfect, it was not nearly so bad for dolls as it would be for us. They talked among themselves and other dolls. They sang and told jokes and stories (Mr Darling was very good at this), and they played Pretend.

Dolls are much better at Pretend than we are, perhaps

because they are made for it. For instance, if you have a Pretend tea party, it is almost always much nicer to have some water or, even better, apple juice for tea and much more fun if there's a real cookie, for a birthday cake, to be cut up. A Pretend gift is not nearly as good as a real one, and certainly if you are hungry it is almost impossible to eat a Pretend meal and feel full up. For dolls it is different. If they are hungry in the morning they have a Pretend breakfast and feel quite satisfied. Most often all their food is Pretend, made of plaster or clay or paper. (Crumpled-up green tissue paper makes excellent salad, for example.) In fact, most dolls prefer Pretend food to real food, as real food can stain them and certainly gets sticky.

Most dolls also Pretend to play musical instruments. I'm sure you have noticed how they love music. Dolls will sit happily for hours, or even days, without moving if they have music to listen to. Mrs Darling played the piano, Mr Darling, the violin and Emma, the harp. Dolls can quite clearly hear Pretend music. They can Pretend to dance, or run races, or even do gymnastics. Revely would Pretend that he climbed out of the case and onto the shelves, where he would pilot the toy bi-planes. Mr Darling had them all Pretend they went for a drive in the lovely toy motor car. He would describe just what they would see on the trip. Once they even Pretended that the car broke down and they all had to walk home.

But while Pretending was fun to the dolls, what they wanted in real life was to be played with. All the dolls in the glass case, from the tiniest baby to the old gentleman doll with a cane, hoped they would leave the shop some day with a child who would love them and play with them often. For if dolls aren't loved and played with, they become stiff and cold. They forget how to talk to each other and how to Pretend and they may even turn into knick-knacks, just useless displays or decorations. In fact, it is considered the greatest insult for one doll to call another a knick-knack. For the greatest tragedy to befall a doll is to remain on a shelf, unloved and alone.

2
Dolls Alone

When all the shoppers went home for tea, the Shopkeeper and her assistant would count the money in the till and tidy the shop.

"My goodness, where does this rubbish come from?" the Shopkeeper would mutter as she swept the floor. There really wasn't much of it, but she was very fussy.

After sweeping up, she would tidy *herself* up while the dolls went nearly crazy with impatience. They could scarcely wait to be alone at last – to stretch themselves, to talk and have fun together. Closing up time was always a very trying time for the toys. There was so much Pretending to be done before morning. Would the shopkeeper *never* leave them in peace?

Sometimes the dolls would tour the doll's houses. And what a lot of different dolls there were! There was the Honourable Elizabeth Joselyn Beeton, an artistocratic little girl doll who came with a brown leather trunk full of beautiful monogrammed clothes. She was the most expensive doll in the shop and also very snobbish. And there was Sir Herbert Banister, an old man doll in an elegant suit, carrying a silver-handled cane. He rather frightened the children, except for Revely, who was quite bold with him and whom he rather liked.

Amanda Miranda liked the animals best, while Revely admired the circus dolls. There were three of them, two men in tights and a beautiful woman covered in spangles, who looked like a ballerina. They were called the Flying Barzinis, and they came together in a box painted with circus scenes. The box also held a trapeze and a net, which the Barzini men despised.

"We don't need no nets," said Michelangelo Barzini, whose grammar was not good at all, but Mrs Darling was far too polite to correct him.

"We fly like birds," said Gianfranco Barzini.

"You break like china," snapped Annamaria Barzini, who loved her brothers but was extremely practical.

Revely wanted to join them and begged Michaelangelo and Gianfranco to take him on the trapeze. But no matter how often he begged, they would not.

"For you it'sa too dangeroso," said Michaelangelo Barzini. "You made of china – break right inna pieces."

The Barzini dolls were not made of porcelain, they were of composition, and although they might break, they would not shatter as Revely and the Darlings would. An accident to a Darling would be dreadful, for though a broken doll can be fixed, a shattered doll is lost forever. No wonder Mrs Darling worried.

"Keep back from the edge," Mrs Darling would admonish the children when they played on the glass-topped counter. "Stay close to the wall," she would call out when they climbed on the shelves.

"Listen to your mother," Mr Darling would say.

"Thank you, Armstead," Mrs Darling would smile nervously. "They take chances. They're in the tall doll's house now and Revely *will* climb on the roof. Please watch them."

Despite the fun they had, all was far from perfect among the dolls. For one thing, there were cliques, and certainly some snobbery at times. Worst was the Honourable Elizabeth Joselyn Beeton, who would play with Enid but not with Amanda Miranda or Revely.

"They are common," she sniffed. "Mass produced. Really, they mustn't come near me. My things are very valuable; who knows what they might do to spoil them?"

This hurt Amanda Miranda but Revely just grinned. He called her Beastly Betty Beeton or just the Beast for short, and this made her very angry.

"You see, I told you Enid," she would huff. "Common." Enid always took their part, but sometimes she would play with the Beast all the same, and that made Amanda Miranda sad.

Perhaps because of this, Amanda Miranda tried to spend as much time as she could on the shelf with the animals. Her favourite was a light-coloured fuzzy Persian cat, and her kitten. Amanda Miranda named the mother cat "Puss" and her kitten "Boots" for its paws were chocolate brown. She kissed them each night. Of all the animals, Amanda Miranda felt that Puss and Boots were hers. They were so soft, and each had a tiny ribbon round the neck. They were so beautifully made that they looked exactly like real cats, but so small that both could fit neatly on a postage stamp.

"You are a most uncommon kitten," Amanda Miranda would whisper to Boots and it would purr loudly.

Often Enid and baby Eugenia played with Amanda Miranda and Puss and Boots. Enid and Amanda Miranda were becoming good friends and spent a lot of time together. Enid didn't like to be stuck with Baby Eugenia, who always got into trouble, but Amanda Miranda didn't mind. She hoped that if she helped Mrs Darling with the baby, Mrs Darling would need her. This might help her to become a Darling. Sometimes, however, a round, jolly nursemaid doll named Mary joined them, pushing Eugenia in a big perambulator.

Of all the dolls, Mary was the children's favourite. In a lovely, lilting voice, she would say, "Two things I like best in the world – hard work and children, that's what I like. I've been a maid of all work as well as a nursemaid, so I can cook, I can clean upstairs or down, I can nurse and I'm not afraid of nothing. Or almost nothing." Amanda Miranda just loved her, even if her grammar was not quite perfect.

Mary told wonderful stories about fairies and leprechauns. She told them the sad stories too of the steadfast tin soldier and the little mermaid. And she told them of the other doll families she had known. For Mary was an antique doll and had lived out in the world. As she rocked the perambulator back and forth, she would talk on and on until Enid and Amanda Miranda, with Boots on her lap, would fall fast asleep. But Mary didn't tell all of her stories to the children.

"It ain't always easy to be a doll out in the Real," she would sometimes say, and shake her head and look sad.

Mary spent a lot of time helping Mrs Darling. They talked and Mrs Darling listened to Mary's tales about the Real and what to expect out there. Mary gave her a lot of good advice.

On rare and special evenings in the toyshop the grown-up dolls would have a formal ball. As all the ladies bustled about getting ready, Amanda Miranda thought Mrs Darling was by far the most beautiful lady doll. And Mr Darling agreed, though he was far too diplomatic to say it when the other ladies could hear.

The children were allowed to dance the first few dances, though Revely would not, no matter what Amanda Miranda promised or threatened. Johnsley made up for it. "I am at your service," he said. Johnsley was romantic and although he was shorter than either of them, he would gallantly alternate between his sister Enid and Amanda Miranda, but she always felt shy and awkward.

"If only my dress was nicer," she thought. "If only it was not so lumpy. And if only my hair was not so wild. I'm afraid I will never become a Darling."

She was not the only one who felt self-conscious and dissatisfied. Emma, too, was uncomfortable. She wasn't old enough to have a beau and there was no one of her own age for her to dance with. The balls made her excited before they began, but during the evening she became sadder and sadder. But though that gave her something to share with Amanda Miranda it did not bring them any closer. Quite the opposite; it made Emma more cross than ever with Amanda Miranda.

For the others, the music boxes tinkled on as the dolls danced into the night. At last all the children dolls would fall asleep, Emma too would begin to doze, and even the grown-up dolls grew weary. Then before dawn broke they would sit and talk about what they hoped might happen when they left the shop. Only Mary would sit alone, watching.

"Who'd ever think I'd become antique," she'd think. "Now I'm so dear I'll probably go to a Serious Collector. Still, I have me memories. And it's surely not all beer and skittles out there in the Real." Then she'd sigh. "Let them have their fun while they can."

3
The American Lady

It was a busy Saturday afternoon when the Darlings were taken out of the case again. This was unusual, because, as the Shopkeeper muttered, "On Saturdays they come to look, not to buy. We ought to call the shop a museum and charge admission. We don't see the Serious Collector on Saturday." It was not surprising that Saturday was Mrs Darling's favourite day.

Because of the crowds, there was a hum all afternoon, a hustle and bustle of exclamations, questions, comments. The shop had the most wonderful doll-sized things, from a string of sausages so small they could be

23

wrapped in a stamp, to a whole bouquet of different flowers which all together were smaller than a rosebud.

"Oh, Mum look at the teeny kitten in the wool basket."

"May I see the little crib and highchair?"

"Katie, come and look at the tiny daffodils in a pot."

"How much is the wicker chaise longue, please?"

"Look, the kettle is smaller than a button, and it really pours and whistles!"

But the largest crowd was always pressed against the glass of the case where the dolls were.

"Oh, look, aren't they sweet!" the mothers and the little girls, and even a few of the boys, exclaimed.

"Yes," the Shopkeeper answered in a crisp, cool voice. "Very fine, and *very* expensive." No one asked to see them.

"Do the doll's houses come assembled?"

"Could we have a look at the flowered rug, please?"

"What's the price of the brass bed?"

By teatime the crowds had thinned, and a plain, brown-haired lady came up to the counter. She was very quiet and went unnoticed. She spent a long time looking over all the furniture and the doll's houses. She peered into the glass case for an even longer time and her eyes came back to the Darlings again and again.

"May I see the doll family?" the lady asked. She spoke with an American accent.

"Of course, Madam," said the Shopkeeper, peering at the lady carefully and approving of her quiet grey wool suit and leather gloves.

She opened the case quickly. "Our highest quality. Very fine indeed."

"Yes, so I see," smiled the American Lady. She

gently lifted up Mrs Darling. "My goodness, aren't you pretty!" she said to her. "And far too young looking to have such a large family. May I have a chair for her, please?" she asked the Shopkeeper, who hurriedly brought out a straight-backed Chippendale dining-room chair.

The American Lady looked at Mr Darling. "You must be very proud of her," she said, as she picked him up in her gloved hand, and Mr Darling realized that he was.

"He's quite tall, isn't he?" she said.

"Perfectly in scale, Madam. An inch to a foot," answered the Shopkeeper primly, while Mr Darling stood up as tall as he could.

The American lady smiled, and began to admire the children.

"Aren't they lovely?" she said.

"Yes, they are the darlings of the shop," said the Shopkeeper.

"Why, what a perfect name for them," the American Lady said. "What do they cost?"

"I'm afraid they are quite expensive, but I could break up the set," said the Shopkeeper. At that moment, Mrs Darling toppled off the straight-backed chair and clattered onto the glass-topped counter.

"Oh, goodness, look what's happened!" said the American Lady. "She's fainted." Carefully, the American Lady picked up Mrs Darling and arranged her on the chair, putting Mr Darling's arm round her. "Now, you take care of her," she admonished gently.

The Shopkeeper smiled tightly. "Very whimsical. But they are very fragile. I am afraid that if they are dropped they will shatter beyond repair. They really

aren't playthings, you know. And, of course, if you damage one, I'm afraid you must purchase it. They need careful handling." At this Mrs Darling shook and nearly fell from her chair again, but this time she fell against Mr Darling.

"We need a child of our own," she said. But of course the two grownups didn't seem to hear her.

"There, there," the American Lady said to Mrs Darling. "You need to be looked after. Don't worry. You are safe with me." She looked up at the Shopkeeper. "It seems a pity to break them up," she said. "They make such a perfect family."

"I could do a bit better on them, if you are a Serious Collector," said the Shopkeeper. The American Lady looked at her calmly. Mrs Darling felt every ounce of her lead-weighted body. Was this lady a Serious Collector?

"I am rarely serious," said the American Lady. The Shopkeeper smiled grimly. "Well, I think I must have them all," the American Lady decided. "Will you take the others out of the case?"

At once, the Shopkeeper became very friendly again and took up Johnsley, Enid, Eugenia and Emma, putting them all on the glass counter. Smiling, the American Lady picked up each one.

"Why, you look just like your father," the American Lady said to Johnsley, whom she had lifted up and held in her glove-covered palm. "I have a feeling that you are a true romantic. You certainly have wonderful curly hair! And you are a very pretty young lady," she said to Emma. "You clearly take after your mother." She called Enid "demure" and admired her smock. Baby Eugenia made her laugh out loud. "Such a mischief! I can tell. My, what a perfect family."

Amanda Miranda, alone in the case with Revely and watching it all, felt as if her heart was breaking. All at once she realized how much she had longed to become a Darling. But it had been a foolish daydream. Her rounded little china body seemed so stiff and hard that it felt as if it would crack. She watched the others through the glass that seemed as thick and cold as the ice of a glacier. They did all look so beautiful, and so fine. She loved and admired them all so much and would miss them so when they left her.

"Oh, Revely," she whispered, "don't feel bad." When Amanda Miranda felt awful, she often tried to distract herself by comforting Boots or her brother. "I love you, Revely. I'll stay with you and take care of you." Though

Amanda Miranda was not a doll made to cry, her vision blurred as if there were tears in her strong, grey eyes.

"I don't care, Amanda," said Revely. "I don't care at all."

"Wait a moment, wait a moment. Where is Amanda Miranda? Where is Revely? Oh dear," said Mr Darling. "This is not right. What about the other children? Are they not included? I must fix this. What can I do?"

"Papa, help them," yelled Enid to him. Johnsley began to cry. (This happens to romantics.) Mrs Darling seemed to stiffen in her chair, and began to concentrate.

While all this was happening, Amanda Miranda felt as if she might fall apart.

"Hah, I told you this would happen, said the Honourable Elizabeth Joselyn Beeton. "You are both so common."

Amanda Miranda and Revely looked up at the Darlings through the glass.

"I don't care," said Revely.

"Oh, *I* do, *I* do," cried Amanda Miranda, who all at once felt very lonely, even with Revely beside her.

"But, what about the others?" asked the American Lady, pointing to Amanda Miranda and Revely. "Let's not forget them."

"Oh, they are not part of the family," said the Shopkeeper primly.

"But we are, we are!" cried Amanda Miranda.

"Hmph," snorted the Honourable Elizabeth Joselyn Beeton.

"They are inexpensive, mass-produced dolls – rather nice for what they are but certainly not of comparable quality," smiled the Shopkeeper.

"We *are* comparable," cried Amanda Miranda.

"They are nowhere near as fine," said the Shop-keeper.

"They *are* as good," said Mrs Darling. She was concentrating very hard.

"But, Mother, they are only mass-produced," said Emma, who was upset and frightened by all that was happening.

"I will see them, please," said the American Lady in a firm voice.

The Shopkeeper made two breaths through her nose, but she lifted Amanda Miranda and Revely out of the case and handed them to the American Lady. Amanda Miranda remembered that her hair was a tangle, and her dress felt lumpier than ever. Revely looked angry.

"If only we had smiles painted on," thought Amanda Miranda. "If only our clothes were sewn, not glued. If only I was finer." The American Lady peered at the two of them.

"You are mistaken. They are clearly part of the family," said the American Lady. "I shall take the lot."

"Oh, we will stay together!" breathed Mrs Darling. Though her body was porcelain and lead, she seemed to go soft all over.

"Oh, Beastly, we are clearly part of the family!" Revely cried.

"Hooray!" yelled Enid, and Johnsley stopped crying at once. This gave him the hiccoughs instead, which was not romantic at all.

Amanda Miranda could hardly believe what was happening.

"Well, it will be an adventure out in the Real,"

Revely said nonchalantly. Revely often tried to act as if he didn't care, even when he cared a great deal.

"Very good, Madam, the eight of them then," responded the Shopkeeper swiftly, for this was a very big sale. "Will you take them with you?"

"No, we shall have them shipped to the United States. Here is the address."

"Oh, dear. The United States!" cried Mr Darling. "We are being sent to America!" It was clear he was very dismayed.

"What is America?" asked Johnsley. "Is it another toyshop?"

"You are so ignorant!" cried Emma. "Of course it isn't a toyshop, it is a nation!"

"Is it bad?" asked Johnsley. "Oh, Mother, is it bad?"

"It is another country across the Atlantic Ocean," explained Mrs Darling calmly. She felt that as long as the family were together, it didn't matter too much where they went. "It is quite a large country, I understand, and there are some lovely places there."

"It is very common," stated the Honourable Elizabeth Joselyn Beeton, who had not been asked.

"Do they have birthdays in America?" asked Enid, practical, as ever.

"Will we like it?" asked Johnsley. "Will we be happy?"

"We shall all be together, and that is the main thing," said Mrs Darling.

And in just a few moments, the dolls were wrapped for shipping. They had almost no time to get used to the idea or bid farewell to their friends.

"Goodbye, Mary. Be well!" cried Mrs Darling. "And thank you."

"Bye-bye Michelangelo, bye-bye Gianfranco! Keep flying!" shouted Revely. "And pooh to you, old Beast." Under his breath he added, "You knick-knack, you." Only Johnsley heard, and he laughed.

"Poor Boots! I'll miss you. Take care of Boots, Puss. Goodbye. Goodbye everyone!" Amanda Miranda waved.

"Bye, all. Good luck!" said Mr Darling just before he was popped into the box.

"Goodbye, goodbye," chorused the dolls in the toy-shop. "Good luck in the Real!"

4
In Transit

Now travelling for dolls, unless they go by pockets, is not at all what it is for people. It is not nearly as interesting because there is no looking out the window, nor the excitement of seeing the train pull up, no leaning over the side of a ferry boat. Usually, dolls are sent in parcels as the Darlings were.

Imagine yourself wrapped in a sheet, surrounded by cushions and placed in the dark in an elevator. That was rather like what happened to the Darlings. They were wrapped in tissue and put in a shallow wooden box, the kind used for very good cigars. The top was fitted on, and all the light and air taped out. It might feel awful to you but it wasn't nearly as bad for the dolls.

Amanda Miranda didn't mind the packing at all. She felt wonderful. She and Revely were clearly "part of the family". She repeated it over and over to herself in the dark, and she believed she had never felt so happy. It was a full feeling, as if her rounded porcelain body was softer and stuffed, instead of hard and hollow. Her chest felt warm and full.

"Children, are you well?" asked Mrs Darling. Everyone said they were.

"Well, don't be afraid," said Mr Darling. "Though it is dark and stuffy, we are all together and we can have a jolly time."

"We are on the way home," said Mrs Darling. And that made Amanda Miranda feel even better.

Once the dolls got used to it, the box was actually very comfortable and cosy, though each of them was wrapped separately and they could neither see one another nor move about.

And so the family talked. Mr Darling made up silly jokes and Mrs Darling told fairy tales and they played games like "Up in the Dollhouse Attic" (which is almost the same as "In Grandmother's Trunk" and is a good memory game.) And they told stories to one another. Johnsley made his up but all the dolls agreed his were the best. "I shall write them down and be an author," he said, though he and all the others knew that doll's don't grow at all. But despite the stories the trip was a long one, and there was much time that they spent quietly.

Mrs Darling kept thinking about the Serious Collector and feeling more than a little bit frightened. Because, as you already know, the worst thing that can happen to a doll is never to be played with and forgotten for weeks and months and years at a time. Then the doll often becomes very lonely. Dolls that have been neglected for too long or that have never been played with at all lose themselves completely. If you go to a museum, look at the antique dolls – some are lively and look right back at you, but others, you may notice, are only the shell of a doll – they don't really seem to be there. These are the poor dolls who were never loved. They have become knick-knacks and are lost forever.

Mary had told Mrs Darling all about getting lost. This is what Mrs Darling was afraid might happen if the American Lady was a Serious Collector and just put them on a shelf. Of course all of the Darlings were curious about her.

"I think she dresses well," said Emma. "For an American." Emma had never seen another American but she thought she sounded quite clever.

"She seems nice, that American lady," said Enid.

"She knew about me," said Johnsley. "I think she is an author, too."

"Don't be silly," sniffed Enid.

"Well, I think she is. And I shall call her by her initials: T.A.L. or Tally for short. We authors do that."

"I like T.A.L.," said Revely. "Tally-ho to America."

"But we must have a child of our own," Mrs Darling said. "That is what we need, children."

"Even you, Mother?" asked Johnsley.

"Even you, mother?" echoed Amanda Miranda. She only repeated it because all at once she felt she *had* to call Mrs Darling, "Mother". Revely never called Mr or Mrs Darling anything at all. But Emma heard and didn't like it when Amanda Miranda called her mother that. She didn't want to share.

Mrs Darling laughed. "Certainly me. And certainly your father," she said to Johnsley, who was about to ask, "All of us?"

"But why?" asked Enid. "Don't you have enough children?"

"Two more than enough," sniffed Emma.

"No, my dear," said Mrs Darling. "I mean a child to play with you and with me and give us life. We all need that."

But Emma's remark, ignored by Mrs Darling, was what Amanda Miranda heard.

"We are not part of the family after all," thought Amanda Miranda, and a great sadness seemed to close in around her in her tissue paper wrapping in the dark. "Perhaps I am not becoming a Darling." Her disappointment felt like a dart in her chest. The paper rustled and seemed to whisper, "not a part, not a part." She seemed to dream, afloat in the blackness. The whispers changed. They said "all apart, all apart, all apart," and Amanda Miranda saw a picture in her

head of herself and Revely spinning and falling and falling, then hitting something hard, breaking all apart into a thousand tiny pieces. It was so real that she cried out.

"What is it?" asked Mr Darling. "Are you all right?" But Amanda Miranda said nothing.

5
Arriving in the Real

At last the time came when the box was shaken about, (which made Amanda Miranda feel funny in her stomach and reminded her of her dream.) Then the top was lifted off. After a moment or two of almost blinding light, the dolls were taken one by one out of the box and set down on a smooth, dark, shiny surface.

"Well, hello," said Tally, for that is how the Darlings had come to think of the American Lady. "I hope you had a comfortable trip." Amanda Miranda looked around. They were in a room rather smaller than the toyshop, and very different. Unlike the cramped and crowded shop this room was spacious and light and almost empty by comparison. They were on a dining table that seemed to the dolls like an enormous, frozen, dark lake – it was so smooth and slippery and wide and long.

"Wicked," exclaimed Revely. "I can really slide on this!"

Mr Darling himself took a bit of a slide and promptly toppled over. Revely and Johnsley and Enid began to laugh for it did look funny, but Amanda Miranda caught her breath and was afraid he was injured. Since her bad dream, she did not like falls at all.

37

"Bit of rum luck," smiled Mr Darling, who liked a joke on himself, and wasn't hurt. But Mrs Darling gasped. They were high on a slippery table top and surrounded by nothing but an edge and a long drop down to a hard parquet floor.

"Do be careful, Armstead" she warned. "No sliding, children."

"My, my, let me help," said Tally, and she picked up Mr Darling. "A bit slippery isn't it? But perhaps you needed the exercise after your journey." And they all did. For, while dolls don't have muscles that cramp, they do become stiff in the joints with disuse. So Tally helped the Darlings to explore the table top and stretch their legs.

The table was round and in its centre there was a pair of silver candlesticks shaped like Greek columns, which flanked a silver basket of fresh flowers. It was a beautiful setting, and as none of the dolls had ever seen real flowers before, they were fascinated, particularly Emma.

"Why, I never imagined anything so beautiful!" she exclaimed. "Look at the colours. And the fragrance. Oh how beautiful!" When you remember that a rose is about the size of a beach umbrella to the Darlings you can imagine how impressive the flowers were. "I wish I could have a picture of one."

Enid, Amanda Miranda and Johnsley ran about and raced each other across the table. Revely was fastest by far.

"I wonder if I could climb up that column," he thought to himself. "That would give me a view." He cleared his mind and imagined himself at the top. Almost as soon as he had thought of it, Tally lifted him up and popped him into the candleholder, like a lookout in a crow's nest.

"Well, now I will be able to make you a bit more comfortable," she said to the Darlings. "I don't have everything you need, but we do have most of the basics here in New York." She left the Darlings for a moment, surrounded by the vast expanse of open table top.

Mrs Darling felt frightened by the immense space and the dangerous edge all round it. But the children were delighted by the air and the light after the cramped box.

Enid lay on her back and squealed, "Oh look! Diamonds in the sky!" Overhead was a crystal chandelier, and though the Darlings had seen tiny doll's house ones, they had never seen a big one lit. It was quite marvellous.

Tally returned with a large cardboard carton and began to take out smaller boxes and pieces of furniture. First she set down two wing chairs with comfortable cushions. They were upholstered in pale yellow, the colour of spring sunshine.

"Perfect for reading the morning paper in," exclaimed Mr Darling, as Tally settled him in the chair. Next, she brought out a divan in the same colour.

"Oh, how lovely!" breathed Mrs Darling, and Tally settled her onto it, throwing a soft, light rug over her.

"I crocheted it myself," she said, almost shyly, and that made Mrs Darling like it even better. (If you are very careful, you can knit on pins for doll's house scarfs and blankets. It isn't easy but it can be done.) "Now, I'm sure you'd like to stretch out on something comfortable tonight, but I'm afraid that you may be a little crowded. However, for the nursery I do have an American invention. It's called a trundle bed."

She lifted out what looked to the Darlings like a huge mahogany raft and put it down on the table beside Johnsley and Enid. It was a high and wide bed, and it was covered in real cotton sheets and a gay calico blanket. At the head were two plump pillows in tiny pillowcases edged in lace – sewn, not glued – and the top sheets were edged with lace as well. Amanda Miranda wanted to put her head down and snuggle in immediately, but the bed held a surprise. Under it was another bed, all made up as well, that pulled out for sleeping and pushed under when it wasn't in use. The dolls had never seen anything like it.

"Ingenious," said Mr Darling. "And the finish on the mahogany looks well done."

"I want to sleep there with Revely," shouted Johnsley. "It's ours."

"I'm afraid I didn't plan for quite so many of you," sighed Tally. "There aren't enough beds, but I don't think you'll mind sharing at first. Revely and Johnsley in the trundle, I think, and the little girls together. And I do have the master bed." She took out a tall four poster with a canopy, made up with fine, soft bedclothes. "I replaced the nasty, stiff ones," she explained. (It's interesting that most doll's furniture does have fabric that is far too stiff and thick. Only a very thin cambric or silk is soft enough to fold naturally on the doll's house scale. That is why Amanda Miranda and Revely's velvet suits were so awkward.)

"I shall have to do a lot more sewing, though. I can see that," said Tally. "We will need more sheets and pillowcases, as well as bedspreads and perhaps some duvets and quilts. And, of course, curtains. Mrs Darling, you and I will have to consult."

Mrs Darling thought of Mary and her household advice and smiled. Things in the Real were far, far better than she had expected and than Mary had led her to believe. She felt exhausted but grateful as well as excited by the idea of a store of good linen, which is indeed a great comfort to any homemaker. (You might try to sew doll's house linens. It is really very easy to make pillows and pillow-slips and sheets, but you must use very fine cotton batiste fabric or else they will be too stiff and heavy. Cotton batiste is expensive, but you only need a very small amount to make half a dozen sheets.)

Next, Tally pulled out a cradle for baby Eugenia. It was mounted on a stand and rocked and all the children wanted to climb in for a ride, (except Emma, of course). Eugenia immediately rocked it so hard it almost overturned. She was a very lively baby. Tally took out more pillows and blankets, which were of the softest flannel and beautifully over-stitched at the sides. She made up a bed on the divan for Emma and in a moment the Darlings were all popped into bed.

"One last thing," said Tally. She opened a very small box with a lid (the kind expensive jewellery comes in) and took out a handful of exquisite doll-sized toys. There was a ballerina doll for Amanda Miranda and a baby doll for Enid. There was a nutcracker for Johnsley and a pull toy horse as well, and for the baby, there was a wonderful goat, rather like a rocking horse, which was mounted on casters and with ribbons of the same shade as baby Eugenia's gown. There was a Raggedy Andy for Revely, but he was not interested.

"Phoo," said Revely. "That's for babies. I'd like a sword."

Tally tucked each toy in beside the dolls and said goodnight, switched off the chandelier and left the room.

So, the Darlings spent their first night in the Real, in comfortable beds on a large slippery table, surrounded by a frightening edge. As Amanda Miranda lay there in the dark, she hugged the toy beside her.

"Perhaps Revely and I *will* be part of the family," she thought. "Perhaps we are safe in the Real."

For a day or two they were left alone, and Mrs Darling began to worry again about whether the American Lady (for only the children called her Tally) was a Serious Collector who would leave them on display. It was lonely for the dolls without the bustle of the shop and no child of their own to play with. Each afternoon a cleaning lady came in, but she was not gentle and kind, as Tally was. She clicked her tongue and shook her head over the Darlings. "Clutter," she called them, and Mr Darling took it as an insult.

Still, the dolls made the best of it and stretched, played, had some time for Pretend. The rest of the time they just waited. But on Saturday Tally did not leave early in the morning. She slept late, then came to the table carrying a basket with a lid.

"Now," she said purposefully, "we've got to do something about these clothes." And she looked hard at Amanda Miranda. Amanda Miranda immediately felt awful again. All the happiness she had been feeling began to drain out of her. She knew at once that despite being bought together and living with the Darlings she and Revely looked different and were not a part of the family. Tally could see it too. Everyone must know. She was very ashamed. Dolls cannot blush (they have no blood, you know, and that is what causes blushing) but she felt just as you would when you are very embarrassed.

"You know, my dear, these simply don't do you

justice. You are a very pretty doll, under these things, and under all that hair."

Amanda Miranda didn't take the compliment; she felt awful. Tally was examining her clothes carefully, turning her over and over.

"Hmm, this is a bit difficult," she said. She reached for Revely and brought him over, too. Revely's suit was of the same grey stuff as Amanda Miranda's. "Well, I'm not sure what I can do," Tally said. "How would you like to be dressed?" she said.

Now, surprising as it may seem, Amanda Miranda had never thought about this. She knew that she hated the ugly grey dress and that it made her feel different and awful. She tried to remember that she was not her dress and tried to know who she was. She had hoped to become part of the family; to become a Darling. That was what she needed. What she had not done was imagine how. And it had never occurred to her to imagine what she wanted instead of the lumpy grey dress.

She became confused and even more embarrassed by Tally. She desperately wanted to change her clothes but she didn't know what she wanted to change into. Perhaps a pink party dress – but that wasn't good to play in, and she did like to run and jump. Maybe a blue velvet – but velvet was so hot and thick – no, not velvet. She simply didn't know what to hope for except that this terrible attention would stop and she would be left alone.

Tally seemed to feel her confusion and set her down gently and picked up Revely again. She turned him over carefully and moved his arms and legs but Revely was stiff and heavy with anger. He knew how Amanda

Miranda felt and at that moment he hated the American Lady. Revely rarely showed it, but he loved Amanda Miranda and wanted her to be happy. He alone was allowed to criticize and pick on her. "Old Tally-ho. Why don't you go?" he rhymed.

"I'm sorry, but I just can't think what to do," said Tally. "I shall have to work on a pattern. I just may not be a good enough tailor!" She set Revely down.

"Pooh, who cares about clothes anyway?" said Revely. "We don't, do we Amanda Miranda?"

"I like your dress as it is Amanda Miranda," chimed in Enid. Usually she was strictly truthful and this was not the truth, but Enid was trying to comfort Amanda Miranda. Amanda Miranda knew that and felt sad.

"Revely and I will never really be part of the family," she thought. "We look different and we feel different and anyone can tell. And Revely will keep on being rude and getting into trouble and no one will want us in the end."

The rest of the day, which Tally spent in unpacking doll's furniture and sewing, was hard for Amanda Miranda.

As the Darlings became used to the Real, they began to live as a family. Each morning Tally left very early and didn't come home until dark, but she did try to leave the dolls in interesting poses, with things to do. This is most important to a doll, who often must be left alone for hours or days at a time. And if dolls move when they are alone they must always return to the same position they were left in. (You might have noticed that sometimes – not often, but sometimes – they forget, and you have found one of your dolls in a different position from the one you left it in.) Mr and Mrs Darling were very strict about returning to the proper position.

Tally sometimes would put Mrs Darling at her desk, with a tiny quill pen and silver inkpot, her stationery laid out before her. Mrs Darling pretended to write to her friends in the toyshop.

Mr Darling might be left in one of the wing chairs, his feet stretched out onto a needlepoint footstool, a tiny newspaper in his hands. (You can cut small sheets from the classified ad section of the paper – the print is just the right size.) Or he would be left to supervise the children at their games. Mrs Darling was very nervous about the edge, and wanted no accidents. Mr Darling was strict about safety, but a good player of games.

Revely was wonderful at games as well. Sometimes they would play hide and seek in the jungle of furniture on the table. Since there were no walls or doors separating the sofa from the beds or the chairs from the bureaus, it was rather like playing in a furniture shop. Sometimes, Johnsley, Enid and Amanda Miranda would play house in one of the cardboard boxes that littered the tabletop. Tally cut a window and door in one and even though it was only the size of your hand, to the dolls it was as big as the crates that appliances come in. Those are, as you probably know, great fun to play with as long as there are no staples or nails to scratch you.

One day Tally came in quite unexpectedly early; so early and so quickly that she found them in new positions. "Being played with by Mrs Shattuck?" she asked. That was the name of the cleaning lady, but Mrs Shattuck did not play with them.

"She gives us flicks," said Enid, talking about Mrs Shattuck's dusting.

"It hurts," said Johnsley.

"She does not like us," explained Amanda Miranda. "We make work for her."

"She is dangerous," murmured Mr Darling to Mrs Darling. "She is rough and careless."

"She does not like us," repeated Amanda Miranda.

"Phoo," said Revely. "I don't care."

Revely wasn't afraid of the cleaning woman, or anything else. Despite warnings he kept sliding on the table top and loved also to inch over to the edge of the table on his belly, then poke his head out over the side. The distance to the floor was so very, very far that it

gave Revely a strange unpleasant feeling, but he was drawn to it again and again. This frightened Amanda Miranda, making her dizzy and reminding her of her terrible dream.

"Oh Revely, don't," begged Amanda Miranda. But he did, and each time Amanda Miranda would creep up beside him to lead him reluctantly away. "Please don't." She was afraid Mr Darling would spy them and be angry. Even more, she was afraid of falling. Revely said he was afraid of nothing.

Revely also climbed to the top of the candlestick and hung several ribbons down from the crow's nest, which the little dolls caught and twined round the column like an old-fashioned Maypole. He directed them from up above, telling them how to weave and duck under each other until all the ribbon was wound into an intricate pattern or a tangled knot – depending on his mood. "I don't know how it gets so tangled," murmured Mrs Shattuck, as she unknotted it each day. She shook her head angrily. Revely laughed.

Revely also invented another wonderful game that the children particularly loved. It was like hide-and-seek but it was much more exciting. They called it "Mr Moon" and in it Revely, for he was always Mr Moon, would climb to the top of the column. Once up there, he sang in a mysterious voice: "Mr Moon is shining down, and he's coming down to eat you up." Of course, the words were nonsense; it was the way Revely sang them that was so exciting. At first, he'd sing in a quiet, calm, mysterious voice, then he would slowly repeat it, getting louder and more fierce and frightening. Amanda Miranda, Enid, Johnsley and Eugenia would shriek and scatter and hide while he slid down the column to look for them. Oh, the terror of hearing him singing his scary Mr Moon song over and over while they crouched behind a chair or under the sofa! Sometimes, Eugenia would become so frightened that she'd burst into tears when Mr Moon found her. This always surprised Revely.

"Phoo!" he said; it's only a game." Eugenia knew that, of course, but sometimes she forgot. So did Johnsley, but he wouldn't cry in front of Revely. And though Revely said "Phoo," he would always pick up Eugenia and give her a piggy-back.

Revely also taught them all to skate. If they balanced on the side of their shoes, the shiny surface was like ice and they could skim along. Amanda Miranda was quite good at it and could do figure eights – backwards as well as forwards. Even Emma joined in the skating. She liked to look graceful.

Often Tally would place them in groups on her bureau or windowledge. Johnsley and Amanda Miranda particularly enjoyed the windowledge, for they loved to look out over the treetops and down at the people in the street five storeys below.

"Look at all the dolls!" shouted Johnsley, the first time he saw them.

"Those are people, silly," corrected Enid. "They are far away so they look small."

"I don't think so," said Johnsley. "I prefer to think they are dolls. It's more romantic."

The best game of all was Revely's masterpiece. He called it foot polo, and it was very rough and wild. All the children would take a croquet mallet and chase after the ball, which was usually a plaster orange or grapefuit. All of them, but one, were in one team – the Keepers – and they only needed to keep the ball on the table top. The other – almost always Revely – was the Shooter, and he would try to knock the ball flying off the edge and into the great space beyond. To hear it drop and echo so far away gave them all shivers, and it filled Amanda Miranda with memories of her horrid dream. When Mrs Darling saw them play the game, she forbade it, unless Emma or she or Mr Darling watched.

"No one near the edge," she would caution again and again.

"Phoo," said Revely. But Amanda Miranda was glad.

Emma, of course, was too big to play these games but she too had found something to do. Tally had given the Darlings a tiny camera, and Emma began to use it.

Her first subjects were the flowers in the centrepiece, which she was shocked at first to see fade and wither. The idea of flowers or anything wilting was new to the dolls. Dolls don't fade.

"I wish they could be preserved," Emma said, and began to take pictures of them. Then she began taking snaps of the family. This interest made Emma easier to be with, though she was always asking the dolls to pose. At least while she was busy with her hobby she did not tease Amanda Miranda.

It wasn't easy for Mrs Darling. "I mustn't always be afraid," she thought. "I must not always worry Armstead and the children." But she was worried. The Darlings were fragile dolls and they were living close to many edges. Because the cleaning lady was careless and because Revely was taking chances and because the children were so lively, Mrs Darling kept on worrying. Mrs Darling had once seen a beautiful porcelain ballerina doll accidentally smashed at the workshop where she was made, and she had never forgotten it. She knew that Revely liked danger and that he sometimes put the others in dangerous situations.

"He has been unhappy and unloved," she said to herself. "He had no mother or father doll to value his safety so he does not value himself. He will learn, but he must be careful. I could not bear it if he shattered. I could not bear it if anything happened to any of them. We need a safe place. Oh, we must hope."

What Mrs Darling needed was a home, a place to live without edges and dangerous heights. Of course, a drawer or a closet would be safe, but it would be awful and dark and lonely. "We could be forgotten and lost that way," thought Mrs Darling. "We need to be seen to be played with. But we need also to be safe."

Sometimes at night she would discuss it with Mr Darling, who tried to comfort her.

"We must hope for a safe home," he said. "There is really nothing more we can do just now."

"You are right, of course. But I worry so. What if . . . well, you know how I worry," said Mrs Darling.

"We can watch the children carefully," said Mr Darling. "I shall be quite stern and we shall all be cautious. And we must keep hoping."

"We are living too near the edge," said Mrs Darling.

During the quiet times, all the dolls were still, dreaming their dreams. Mr and Mrs Darling hoped for a home. Emma hoped to be happier and not feel so unkind at times. She often felt guilty about how she acted. Johnsley dreamed of the books he would write, and the other children had children's dreams, except Amanda Miranda.

"Perhaps, some day I can truly be a Darling." It was all she wanted. "If only I could keep us all safe, then they would need me." And so she watched the other children carefully to make sure they didn't fall into harm's way.

One quiet evening the silence was broken by the buzzer, announcing a delivery. Tally rushed to the door and a huge crate was wheeled in by the porter. He set it in the Darlings' room, beside the big table.

"Could you help me open it up?" Tally asked the porter.

It was not an easy job and took some time. The porter used a crow bar to prise off some outside boards and pulled out several long, sharp nails. But at last the packing case was dismantled, and the packing straw revealed.

"I think it is a motor car," said Johnsley, who dearly loved motor cars, but it was far too big a box for a toy car.

Tally kept picking up handfuls of straw and stuffing it into a bag until at long last the dolls could see what was in the box.

"Oh my goodness!" cried Amanda Miranda. "It's our doll's house!"

6
The Doll's House Arrives

The house was splendid. "Exactly what I hoped for," said Mr Darling. "A very grand house indeed."

"It's beautiful," breathed Amanda Miranda.

"It's big," said Revely, "and it's got a lovely roof to climb on."

All the dolls began to point out things they could see. All the dolls felt they had imagined such a house, and now it was here. Only Mrs Darling was silent.

The house was three storeys tall, with a pitched grey roof. The door was white and flanked on either side by white flowers in clay pots. There were also window boxes planted with flowers, a tiny brass doorknob, a brass knocker and a letterbox. "Exactly what I wished for," repeated Mr Darling.

It was a warm pinkish-brown colour, with white trim on the windows. It opened at the front, rather like a cabinet and when it had been opened, the Darlings could see that there were two rooms on each floor, and a hall with a staircase up the centre.

"Kitchen and dining room downstairs, then library and drawing room, then master bedroom and Emma's room, then nurseries under the eaves," Tally explained. "It's a New York town house, just what a family like

yours would live in if you had moved to New York. You may be a bit crowded, but it will be better than the table top. It *is* lovely, I must say."

But, while the Darlings had been excited by the outside which did look beautiful, the inside of the house was bare and empty. The rooms were like boxes, the walls and floors unpainted, the stairs uncarpeted, the wood raw. In fact, the inside of the doll's house looked very like the inside of the box the Darlings had been shipped from London in.

"Oh, my," said Mr Darling when he saw the inside. "What is wrong with the house? It's all wrong inside. Why, it's just an empty crate."

"Oh, I so wanted a real room of my own," said Emma.

"It's like the box we were shipped in," cried Revely.

"I hate it!" Enid exclaimed.

"Me, too," chorused Johnsley, who very nearly began to cry.

Amanda Miranda felt disappointed also. It certainly didn't look like the house she had hoped for.

But Mrs Darling, at first very quiet, became cheerful. "Now, now," she said in a comforting way. "This is just a beginning. Don't lose hope. Making a home takes time, and work. This is only the first step. We're on the way home."

"But there are no fireplaces, no parquet floors," said Mr Darling. "I can't lean against the mantelpiece with my back to the fire!"

"There are no doors to swing on," said Revely.

"It's just a box," said Enid, who was quite literal.

"There's no paper on the walls. There are no curtains at the windows," cried Emma brokenly.

"There is no motor car, none at all," said Johnsley. "I would see it if there was."

"There are no banisters on the stairs to slide down," said Revely.

"It's just a box," repeated Enid.

"Yes, but it closes and it is safe, that is the most important thing. There are no edges. It closes up. The rest will come if we work at it," replied Mrs Darling. "You must keep hoping. And we must work at this." She sighed with contentment. For the first time since they left the toyshop, she felt they might really be safe. When the house was closed and latched, there were no edges at all. They would truly be safe inside.

"Children, listen to your mother," said Mr Darling.

"But what can we do?" asked Emma. "I so wanted a room of my own with a window seat and a dark room to develop my pictures."

"Things are not so important as all that. Things are only things and we can do without many of them. All we really need is to be safe and together. Now if we have faith and keep a clear idea of what we need, we will get it," Mrs Darling replied. She was greatly relieved.

But she still worried because there were no children to play with them. "Yet I think I am beginning to trust this American Lady and I choose to believe it will all be fine. She kept us all together and now she has provided us with a house and once we are inside there are no edges to fall off. I will be so glad to get off the bureau and the table top and the windowledge."

"Well, at least I can climb on the roof leads," said Revely cheerfully.

"You can, but you may not," said Mrs Darling,

who even in her extreme relief remembered her grammar. "Revely, you must take care of your speech and yourself."

"I'm confused," said Revely. "What do you mean?"

"She means you will be a very sorry little boy doll if you climb on the roof," said Mr Darling sternly. "There will be none of that." This comforted Amanda Miranda, who had become very nervous at the thought of roof-climbing.

"But may we slide down the banisters?" asked Johnsley. He imagined a very exciting life in the house with Revely, swinging on doors and sliding down banisters. He wasn't sure exactly what banisters were, and imagined them to be something like a combination of the old Sir Herbert Banister doll in the London toyshop and the stuffed boa constrictors. Still, he knew if Revely wanted to slide on them, he did too.

"As soon as we have them, you may," smiled Mr Darling.

Revely thought it would be fun to bump down the stairs on a tray, rather, like sledging indoors, but he decided not to mention it. And perhaps he could sledge on the floors if he could get hold of Mrs Shattuck's soap flakes. He also was determined to explore the roof, no matter what he was told. For one thing, it was because he was adventurous and for another, it was because Revely liked Mr Darling to notice him, even if it was because he misbehaved.

"Well," Tally said, "the house came from a wonderful American toyshop and you all seem to approve. Of course, fixing the house up will be a lot of work, and will take time, but I thought this way we could get it exactly as you wanted. Oh, and something else has arrived." She bent over a smaller box and removed something wrapped in layers of newspaper and tissue paper.

"You will surely need some help, Mrs Darling, and here she is." The last sheet of tissue paper dropped off and Mary, the nurserymaid doll, stood revealed, her rather pudgy face beaming.

Amanda Miranda's doll heart jumped. Dear Mary from the toyshop had joined them!

"Welcome, Mary!" Mr Darling cried. All the children shouted their greetings. They were so glad to see her.

"Was the trip very hard for you, all alone?" inquired Mrs Darling.

"Well, I wasn't quite alone," smiled Mary. And as she spoke the American Lady unwrapped a little tissue package disclosing a tiny Persian cat and her kitten.

"Puss!" cried Amanda Miranda. "Oh, and Boots too!" and she could say no more.

"And fine furry felines they is," said Mary. "They was good company, but faith, it was a long trip! Still, t'wasn't the longest I've taken, nor to the worst destination either. Is that our new house? Not too bad. Hope the kitchen is large. You all look well, though. Seems to agree with you, out in the Real."

7

The Work Begins

Mary had lots of news to report from the toyshop.
The Barzinis were well, were working on a new trick
and had had no accidents. The Honourable Elizabeth
Joselyn Beeton was still snobbish and still not taken
home by anyone. "And never will be, the Beast,"
muttered Revely. Old Sir Banister also remained.

"People aren't silly – they chose us, and they can
tell how sour the Beast is," said Revely.

Several new dolls had arrived, but no complete

families. Amanda Miranda asked about the animals, and Mr Darling wondered about his violin, and the questions and the news went on and on.

At last, after she had kissed and hugged all the children, except Revely, who squirmed away, Mary looked at the furniture on the table top and the newly unwrapped house. She smiled. "It seems I got here just in time. Well, there's nothing I like better than hard work – except children."

Afterwards, Mrs Darling remembered the time of working on their house with very tender thoughts. Each day the American Lady left for work, leaving them in the house. That first afternoon, Mrs Shattuck came in and saw the mess from the packing case. "Tch, tch, tch." She made the noise with her teeth like an angry clock as she cleared up the wrappings.

"Who is she?" asked Mary.

"She is the housekeeper," answered Mrs Darling.

"No she's not. She's just a cleaning lady. I know her kind," Mary said. "Often a problem."

But there were no problems at first in the house. They were safe to pretend and play and plan and hope. Of course, it wasn't as good as really being played with by a child of their own, but it was pleasant enough. After dinner the American Lady would work on the house, and often she would unwrap some new addition.

First there was the painting and papering. She brought many wallpaper samples and tried them on the walls. Mrs Darling would stare seriously at them. So would the American Lady, and by this process, a soft yellow moiré was selected for the parlour, a cheerful blue striped paper for the kitchen, a warm red paint for the library and a pretty print for Mr and Mrs Darling's bedroom. She was so busy with the house that she almost had no time to worry. But still, Mrs Darling in her few spare moments thought about getting played with.

"The decor is lovely, but will there be a child?" she wondered.

Emma and Amanda Miranda helped to choose colours and patterns. Emma badly wanted her own room, for her photography took up more and more space. In fact, she was quite certain that she *had* to have a room for herself and her equipment. But there was a problem about that, because it seemed that Amanda Miranda had no place to go.

"The little boys can be in the north attic, and Enid, Eugenia and Mary in the south," planned Tally out loud. "That will put the master bedroom, bath and Emma on the second floor and her closet can be a dark room. The drawing room and library are on the first floor, and the kitchen and dining room on the ground floor, beside the conservatory. It should work."

But where, wondered Amanda Miranda, would *she* sleep?

"It better not be in my room," said Emma. She had not been too cordial to Amanda Miranda, but she had not been too awful either. Now, however, she was cold.

Often at the weekends Tally would take some of the dolls on an excursion to the American toyshop. This was a huge and magnificent one. It was very different from the small, dark toyshop in London because it was so big and it seemed to have almost every toy in the world. The doll's house department was particularly wonderful, with beautiful houses, wonderful furniture and the finest accessories.

Mrs Darling almost always went with the American Lady and with her would go some of the children, each taking turns. This was a very special treat. Once in the shop, the American Lady went straight to the doll's house department, and the dolls would look at almost everything imaginable in tiny, tiny scale. Doll's house scale is usually one inch to one foot, although some doll's houses are smaller and some larger.

And what wonderful things there were! Mrs Darling selected furniture – a dining room table and eight chairs, a sideboard to go with it, a large gilt mirror, even a little potty seat for Baby Eugenia. When Mary came along, they often bought kitchenware: copper pots and kettles, all smaller than a sewing thimble, tiny mixing bowls that nestled one inside another, porcelain serving plates, and a teapot that could pass through Tally's ring.

One brilliant day, the American Lady brought home a larger than usual carton. "I'm certain you will enjoy this," she said to Mr Darling. "You will, as well, I think," she added, bringing Johnsley and Revely to the table. "There." She unwrapped the box and pulled out a wonderful motor car with headlamps and brass, and a front seat and a curving round back seat and a rumble seat as well.

"Can I drive it?" Revely asked at once.

"Certainly not," said Mr Darling. "But you may blow the horn. What do you think, Johnsley? Would you like to go for a ride?" Johnsley nearly cried with happiness.

Like the motor car, most of the things Tally bought were very fine and some were quite expensive, but she didn't seem to mind. Mrs Darling remembered the Shopkeeper in London saying: "Only Serious Collectors spend lots of money." And she would worry. For while Mrs Darling loved the beautiful things, she feared being collected. "I must keep hoping we'll be played with," she thought. "We need to be played with."

Slowly the house began to take shape and each of the dolls found their special place. For Amanda Miranda, it was on the leather Chesterfield sofa in the library. "I can look out and see the ivy running up the front of the house." She played there with Boots while Puss napped. Somehow it made her feel safe.

For Enid, it was in the alcove under the stairs. "Come and see my house and come to my tea party," she would say. She had her own dolls and a tiny table-and-chair-set that was just their size. Amanda Miranda was invited often and usually Johnsley would come as well, though Revely scorned tea parties.

Johnsley loved the stairwell. "It is mysterious and lonely and safe all at the same time," he explained. Here he sat with his toys up and down the steps. He played motor car driving, or pirates, or sometimes school, with the toys as his pupils. He was a very strict teacher and frequently kept them after. Often he wished for a special friend to play with on the stairs, and so he invented Bayruth, a bear, that was sometimes a boy bear and sometimes a girl bear, depending on his mood. "That is why he is called Bayruth. It's both kinds of name in one."

For some reason Enid didn't like this idea. "May Bayruth come to tea?" asked Johnsley.

"Ruth is a girl's name, but Bay isn't a boy's. It is altogether a stupid name," said Enid. "Anyway he isn't real so he can't come."

"Bayruth says you are very disagreeable," said Johnsley.

For Revely, the special place was the roof. This was dangerous, but he managed very often to be left there by the American Lady, or at least close to the window where he could get out there easily enough. Revely, remembering the Barzinis, had a plan involving some string, the two chimneys on either side of the roof, and a bicycle. It was very dangerous; so dangerous in fact that even Revely was thinking twice about it. To tell the truth, as Revely started to feel safer and more wanted, he was not feeling the need to do such dangerous things.

Baby Eugenia, who managed always to get into mischief, adored the bathroom, where she loved to pull the towels out of the racks, and the kitchen, where she'd often sit on a high chair and play at the table with flour and water, making an awful mess. (If *you* make doll's house dough, use flour and water and salt – this makes it less sticky.) Enid played too, and sometimes Amanda Miranda joined them and they braided little loaves of bread.

One day, the American Lady brought home a stove, and it thrilled Mary so much she was speechless. It wasn't a modern stove but a big white enamel box with four burners and a baking oven and a griddle and a drying oven. It even had a place to put plates to warm. Though it really couldn't have a fire in it, which would be too dangerous in a doll's house, it did all the pretend cooking any doll could hope for. When Tally brought it out, Mary's eyes shone and she immediately got busy cutting up a raspberry and rolling out dough for a pie. One raspberry made one perfect pie with just enough left over for Enid to make a tiny pie of her own.

The kitchen also had a white enamel sink and a pinewood kitchen cupboard that Mary called a "safe". There was a tiny wooden breadbox that had a sliding top, like a desk, that closed and opened. Tally put a plaster loaf inside. There was a deal table, the top about the size of a playing card, that Mary scrubbed and scrubbed. There were kitchen chairs the children sat on at breakfast, and, in the corner, was a comfy armchair with a cushion and an afghan, each square a different colour and each one smaller than a buttercup leaf. This was where Mary sat in the few moments she wasn't busy, and where she put her feet up on an over-turned tub. But she had to share her spot with Buster, the kitchen cat. He curled up in her lap, purring as she sipped her tea.

"Working like a horse," she grumbled with a smile. "And looking after all those children. An old antique like me! And I expected a rest after all these years. Well, isn't the Real surprisin'!"

Mr Darling claimed the library as his own, and spent much of his day there. He was busy poring over floor plans and different samples of wood – moulding, wainscotting, skirting boards, doors and door frames as well as hardware like door knobs, hinges, brackets, and all sorts of other bits and pieces that fascinated Revely. Mr Darling patiently explained the names of all the

pieces: corbels and cornices and lintels. Revely loved
the sound of the architectural parts and used to repeat
them like a poem: "corbels and cornices and lintels."

"Well, my dear," said Mr Darling one afternoon,
as he joined his wife in the conservatory, "we do
appear to have landed on our feet here in the Real."
His own feet were crossed comfortably on the chaise
longue. Puss lay in the sunshine on the tiled floor.
Mrs Darling was writing a shopping list at the little
white wicker desk. "Apart from that rather nasty piece
of work, Mrs Shattuck, we are quite well off."

"Yes, Armstead, but don't you think it odd that there
is no child to play with us? What will happen when the
house is finished? The American Lady is kind, but she
won't play with us. Grownups don't play, do they? Will
we just gather dust? I am afraid we are being collected
and will all be lost."

"Oh, my dear, I do not think so. All is going
so well. The house will be beautiful, and keep us all
safe. So far, she has not forgotten us or put us away.
And I am hoping she has a daughter or son who will
play with us."

"But where are they? We haven't seen any children.
Isn't it strange?"

"My dear, I cannot say. Perhaps they are at school.
We can only know what we need, do the best we can,
and hope for it. Worry does no good."

"You are right, Armstead, but I cannot help it
sometimes. I love you and the children so much. We
just *must* have a child of our own to play with us."

"And I agree and I love you, but worrying will
do no good. It just makes you tired and cross."

At that moment, Mary entered the conservatory, bringing a tray of afternoon tea. Of all the meals, tea is the nicest. Because they were English dolls, the Darlings couldn't do without tea, and the whole family would gather to pretend to eat their bread and butter, tiny sandwiches, scones and cakes and tarts.

The youngest children only had milk with a teaspoon of tea in it, Amanda Miranda had half tea and half milk, and Emma had real tea. They all sat together in the conservatory each fine afternoon and took tea together. On wet or gloomy days, they took tea in the library. Amanda Miranda always kept a saucerful of cream for Boots, who often stepped in it.

"Oh, at times like this I think we are the luckiest dolls in the world," said Mrs Darling with a sigh.

"I quite agree with you, my dear," said her husband. "Revely, would you please stop trying to balance your teacup on your forehead?" Revely stopped, but Johnsley felt inspired to try, then Enid. There was an epidemic of china juggling until it was time to return to the work of making their home. Mr Darling went to hang a painting in the library, with help from Johnsley, while Mrs Darling, Mary and Amanda Miranda did more unpacking. Slowly, room by room, the house stopped looking like a cold, unfriendly wooden box and was becoming a warm and beautiful home.

Revely was a particularly good handyman and helped to put all the doorknobs on. Since there were sixteen doors in the house, this was a lot of work.

"Be careful not to scratch the paint on my door," said Emma as Revely worked on it. "I especially want a lock so I can keep undesirables out."

Revely knew that doll's house doors have no locks, and he knew Emma knew it too. it was her way of saying, "keep away". Amanda Miranda overheard her and she understood it also.

8
Cat's Cradle

Sometimes the Darlings had a break from working on their house, when Tally would put them all in the motor car, which really ran, and would send them for a drive.

"She almost remembers how to play," said Mrs Darling gratefully. "She knows what we need. How very odd for a grownup. It is better than nothing, but it makes me long even more for a child of our own."

Revely and Johnsley both wanted to sit in the front beside Mr Darling. Revely watched carefully as Mr Darling worked the clutch and the brake and turned the wheel.

In the back were all the girls and Mrs Darling, holding baby Eugenia on her lap.

"It is very crowded," complained Emma.

"I'm sorry," said Amanda Miranda. "Should I move?" But Tally had pressed the switch and the motor car fairly flew over the floor, thrilling them all.

Sometimes Tally put a picnic hamper in the rumble seat, and the Darlings had tea out. Once it was on the windowsill, and once on a bookshelf. Once they nearly stopped at the telephone table, but there was a heat grating there in the floor that frightened Mrs Darling.

"You could slip into it and be lost," she said to the children. "And if the American Lady did not find you . . . well, let's just not stop." They drove on.

The motor car went very fast; they felt the breeze on their faces as they watched the scenery flash by.

"Oh, this is exciting," cried Amanda Miranda.

"Hold my hand," screamed Enid, laughing.

"Oh, my hair," moaned Emma, but her cheeks looked pink and excited, and she was smiling. Baby Eugenia laughed with joy.

It was one morning after such a trip that Mrs Shattuck came in early. The American Lady had gone out, and Mrs Shattuck was in a very flicking mood.

"Ouch," cried Revely, as Mrs Shattuck dusted the roof and flicked him as he sat at the window.

"Ouch," cried Emma, who was at the front door when she was flicked with Mrs Shattuck's duster.

"Oh, my," gasped Mr Darling, when Mrs Shattuck put her big duster into the library and knocked him over.

Amanda Miranda was sitting on the leather sofa trying to knit with two pins. Puss was beside her, and tiny Boots balanced on the sofa arm. Mrs Shattuck's rough hand wiped down the window, then stopped. Putting down the cruel dust flicker, her eye went from Amanda Miranda to Boots. Pushing two fingers through the open window, she picked him up.

"Leave my kitten alone." Amanda Miranda did not like Mrs Shattuck at all, but of course the cleaning lady heard nothing and would not have paid any heed if she had.

At that moment the telephone rang. Mrs Shattuck jumped at the sound, then went to the phone, holding tiny Boots in her hand. Boots did not like Mrs Shattuck either, or perhaps she pinched him, but in any case, I think he scratched her. Of course it was only as big a scratch as a kitten the size of a collar button could give, but as Mrs Shattuck answered the phone, her hand jumped from the scratch and Boots sprang free, only to drop to the floor and through the heat grating. Amanda Miranda clearly heard him fall.

"Oh Puss! What shall we do?" Puss meowed piteously and Amanda Miranda began to cry.

Mrs Shattuck was talking on the phone and writing a message. When she hung up, she squatted down to find Boots, but he wasn't on the floor. "Tch, tch," she said, and got up, shaking her head.

"She isn't going to get him! She is leaving him there!"

"Nasty knick-knack," said Revely from his window perch. Of course, it was silly of him to call someone in the Real a knick-knack, but it was the worst word he knew.

Enid and Johnsley heard. "What shall we do?" they cried. Mother and Mary had gone off with Tally and Father had been knocked over by Mrs Shattuck. He did not answer. Amanda Miranda began to cry.

"He'll be lost. Oh poor Boots." She thought she could hear him meowing faintly. "Oh poor Boots."

"Come on then," said Revely. "We've got to get him." From under his bed, he began uncoiling string that was as thick as a rope to the dolls. He had been saving bits from unwrapped packages to make a tight-rope, and now he threw one end out of the window, tying the other to the bed.

"I'm going to climb down," he said. "Johnsley, you're the smallest, you'll have to come too. Amanda Miranda you're heavy. Sit on this bed and keep it from moving. Enid, look out of the window and keep an eye out for that big old knick knack. Yell if you see her. Come on Johnsley. You can do it, can't you?"

"Oh yes!" Johnsley shouted. "And Bayruth too." In just a moment, the two little dolls were out of the window and sliding down the string to the ground. Once there, Revely walked to the motor car.

"We shall have to drive," he said calmly. "It's

too far to walk, and Mrs Shattuck might tread on us if we're on the floor."

"But should we?" asked Johnsley.

"It is the only way," said Revely. "I've watched Father. I know how to drive."

In a moment they were in the motor car and Revely kicked the starting switch. He let out the clutch and they were off, flying across the floor on their rescue mission.

Johnsley will never forget those moments. "It was wonderful," he said later. "Like being a highwayman and the cavalry and flying all at the same time. Bayruth was a little frightened but I told him it was all right. Some day I shall write a play about it and call it *The Mission to Liberate Boots*."

The most dangerous part of the mission was when they had to stop at the heat grating. Revely had to kick the switch and steer at the same time and it wasn't easy.

He missed the first time round and had to go all around the dining room again as he wasn't strong enough to make a U-turn.

"Hold on, Johnsley," he yelled. "I'm going to try to stop!" And this time he did.

Enid watched from the window while they got out of the car, ran to the grating and looked in. Johnsley waved to her. Then Enid gasped.

"Amanda Miranda," she shouted. "Revely is lowering Johnsley into the grating head first!" Amanda Miranda shivered. "Oh, it's all right, he's pulled him out by his feet, but he's all dusty. He doesn't have Boots. Wait, he's gone in again. He's out. He's out and he has your kitten."

They were in the car and on their way back in a moment. It was only another moment till they tied a knot round Boots and Amanda Miranda and Enid hoisted him up. Then they did the same with the other two, which was much harder. But even Emma joined them and helped.

"We've done it," shouted Johnsley. "We all did it together."

"Oh, thank you," Amanda Miranda said. She hugged Boots tight.

Of course, when Mrs Darling came home and Mr Darling recovered there was much discussion and scolding.

"You were brave and thought quickly but you must be more careful," Mrs Darling said.

"But I'm glad we did it," said Revely, and he felt proud.

"Me too," echoed Johnsley. "And so is Bayruth."

Emma took a portrait shot of the two heroes, and

another photo of Puss grooming Boots, who, aside from being dusty, acted as if he went down heat gratings daily. Both photos came out well.

"Oh, Boots," was all Amanda Miranda could say.

9
Settling In

At last virtually everything was finished: the floors
were tiled in the kitchen, conservatory and bathroom,
or varnished in the dining room, drawing room and
library and covered with rugs in the bedrooms. The
walls were painted or papered. Pictures were put up.
(Stamps make excellent doll's house pictures.) Electric
lights were installed. Mouldings were painted, doors
were hung, furniture was placed, mantelpieces were
dusted (there were four fireplaces). The house was
ready for the Darlings.

Amanda Miranda thought it couldn't be more perfect. Beside each fireplace there were baskets of logs (really only tiny twigs, but log-sized to the Darlings). There were window boxes filled with flowers, soap on the shelf by the sink, towels on the towel rack, dishes in the dish rack and bread in the breadbox. There were tiny hatboxes in Mrs Darling's wardrobes, a pocket watch on Mr Darling's bureau, toys in the toybox in the south nursery, runners on the stairs, ferns in the pots, and perfume bottles on the dressing table in Emma's room. "Everything has been thought of, except a child of our own," sighed Mrs Darling. "Everything has been thought of but that."

But that was not the only thing missing.

"Where do I belong?" whispered Amanda Miranda to Boots.

Tally hadn't exactly mentioned her, and Amanda Miranda was afraid to ask Mrs Darling and afraid to hope for anything. She wanted a place, a special place, and she was too old for the nursery. Sharing a room with Emma would be perfect but she didn't want Emma to be angry. Emma did seem a little calmer. She had her camera. She had also found a tiny book about cameras and was always busy taking pictures. And in the evenings she played the harp in a trio with her father on the violin and her mother at the piano. Yet still Amanda Miranda was nervous. Sometimes looking at Emma she would remember her dream and almost feel that she was spinning off the edge again, out of control.

All this time the Darlings, except when they were working on the house, had been living on the table top, surrounded by the dangerous edge, exposed to draughts and with no privacy. All of them had longed for smaller spaces, and doors and walls and ceilings overhead. Living on a table top was rather like living on a high bare plateau. And Amanda Miranda hoped that when they were in their house she'd at last feel she was part of the family.

"But perhaps Revely and I are common," she said to herself, and didn't know what to do. So she held Boots closer and thought and thought.

"I know," she said to the kitten, "I'll be useful. If I work hard, and they need me, Revely and I will be allowed to stay." Once she had this idea, she was always the first to run an errand or fetch something or untangle a string. Amanda Miranda was far from lazy. She did a great deal of work on the new house: she helped to paint all the skirting boards and swept up all the scrap pieces of wallpaper and wiped up spilled glue. She was useful to Mary and helped with her work. She was helpful to Mrs Darling with her sewing and mending, and she wound all her wool (which in doll's houses is embroidery thread). She also fed and combed Buster the kitchen cat as well as Puss and Boots and helped look after baby Eugenia whenever the others were occupied.

But Amanda Miranda was a little girl doll, not an adult doll, and little girls, and boys too, need playtime. Although she tried to work and work to deserve to belong to the Darlings, she needed just as much to play and have time just to be herself.

One afternoon, Emma was minding Eugenia while Mrs Darling and Mary were busy putting up preserves.

Emma was exasperated because she had some flowers she wanted to photograph, waiting for her in the conservatory, and Eugenia simply couldn't be trusted in there, as there were so many ways to get into mischief. Baby Eugenia was especially talented in getting dirty, losing buttons and breaking things, which is perfectly normal for a two-and-a-half-year-old doll. Actually, baby dolls are a bit easier than real babies because at least Emma didn't have to worry about her eating small objects.

"Oh, Eugenia, why must I waste my day on you!" Emma exclaimed impatiently, though she only half meant it.

"I'll mind her," volunteered Amanda Miranda. "We could play house."

"Oh, that would be splendid!" Emma exclaimed. "It wouldn't be for too long. I have some things I want to do. But you will be careful of her."

"Certainly! I am very responsible," answered Amanda Miranda. And she was.

At first she had fun. She made a puppet show for Eugenia and then she brought her to the nursery where Enid was playing school. But Eugenia kept upsetting the classroom and Enid begged Amanda Miranda to take her away. Next they went into the boys' room where Eugenia jumped on the brass cots (which had metal springs and were very bouncy indeed), but she annoyed Johnsley who was playing at being an author and needed quiet. Then Amanda Miranda took her on the stairs, but Eugenia would try to slide on the banister and Amanda Miranda was afraid she would fall.

Feeling nervous, Amanda Miranda took her to the bedroom landing where Eugenia stood on a chair and made faces in the mirror, but she kept trying to grab at her reflection, so Amanda Miranda took her away before she broke the glass.

By now, Amanda Miranda was rather desperate. She decided to take Eugenia into the bathroom. This was an old style room with a mahogany and porcelain tub, a pull chain W.C. and brass taps on the sink and bath. The water did not run but the taps did turn.

Eugenia immediately pulled the towels off the racks. Amanda Miranda told her to be still and sit down, which Eugenia did, and for a while she listened to a story Amanda Miranda made up on the spot about a lonely rubber duck that wanted to be a champion diver. Then Eugenia lay down on the cool tiles and said she wanted a blanket, so Amanda Miranda hopped up and ran to fetch one, hoping Eugenia would take a nap.

Now, you probably know that that was a mistake because babies should never be left alone, even for a minute. Babies just naturally get into trouble and Baby Eugenia had a particular talent for it. She decided, in Amanda Miranda's absence, that she too wanted to be a diver like the duck, and she crawled near the tap, balanced on one foot and was about to dive head first into the empty bathtub. Just then, Emma walked in.

"Oh my goodness," she yelled. "Stop. Don't you dare move." She grabbed Baby Eugenia and hugged her tight. "What were you doing? You could have broken yourself!"

"Manda told me to," said Eugenia, because she was frightened and knew she was in trouble.

Well, you can imagine the scene when Amanda Miranda returned a moment later. Emma yelled and called her a bad, lazy, dangerous doll, and when

Amanda Miranda tried to explain, Emma wouldn't listen. Eugenia started to cry and kick and became upset. Amanda Miranda talked louder and louder, hoping Emma would hear.

"I didn't mean it. It was an accident. I only left her for a moment."

"You told her to dive into the tub! Wait till I tell Mother! She won't want you in this house and neither do I." Emma was angry, badly frightened, and felt guilty because *she* had left the baby for so long. Clutching Baby Eugenia, she stalked downstairs.

Amanda Miranda sat down hard on the top step. Somehow, whatever she did, it went wrong. She felt awful.

Revely crept up behind her. "I heard the yelling,"

he said. "What happened?" His porcelain face looked very pale and serious and matched his sister's perfectly.

So Amanda Miranda explained how it had been her fault, leaving Eugenia alone, and how Emma was blaming her.

"She shouldn't have left you alone with the baby so long," said Revely, which was true. "It's all her fault," he added, which wasn't true, but it made him feel better. He had overheard Emma say that she would tell Mrs Darling and that Amanda Miranda would be put out. Although he wouldn't admit it, it scared him too.

"If you go, I go, Amanda," he said. "We don't care, do we?"

"But I do, Revely, I do care," cried Amanda Miranda. "I really, really do. I'm going to Mother to apologize." And she got up and walked down the stairs, leaving Revely alone.

"I don't care," Revely said to himself. He said this when he cared the most. Since he had rescued Boots he had been feeling happy. But Emma had ruined it. "Emma thinks she's so fine. Well, not so fine to me. And everything has to be so perfect, but she's not so perfect." Revely's feelings were hurt and that made him angry. And when he was angry he got ideas that were sometimes dangerous. He was thinking about one now.

"I don't care," repeated Revely. "I really don't."

10
Bad Things Get Worse

Emma spent the rest of the morning in the conservatory photographing her mother potting some plants. She had already forgotten her anger at Amanda Miranda. She had been frightened when she saw Eugenia on the bathtub, and reacted with anger. This is very natural behaviour. (Perhaps you have stepped off a curb without looking and your mother has pulled you back angrily and scolded. It is because she was frightened

84

for your safety and getting angry gets the fear out.)

Amanda Miranda felt sad, but she knew that she had been wrong. She made a mistake, and she needed to make it all right. In her heart she knew Mrs Darling would forgive her.

It was Revely who was most upset. He had over-heard Emma and come to save Amanda Miranda and she hadn't joined him. Revely was angry. He had an idea. "I don't care," he said again, and stealthily crept up the stairs to Emma's room, a brush and paint tin in his hand.

The morning was quiet. Mary was making the beds in the nurseries and Enid was helping while Eugenia helped by bouncing on the bed. Mr Darling was looking over some bills in the library.

It happened when Mrs Darling decided to re-pot a lily plant and Emma went up to the bedroom to fetch more film. As she opened the door, she saw Revely and screamed. He had climbed onto her dressing table and in black paint, left over from the door trim, was scrawling, "Emma is a knick-knack" on her beautiful wallpaper. He was almost finished, but hearing her scream behind him and seeing the flash of her camera – Emma had pushed the shutter without meaning to – startled him so that he dropped the paintbrush, tripped over the paint tin, lost his balance and overturned a beautiful chair. He fell, and the chair leg cracked off with a nasty splintering sound.

"Oh no! Just look what you have done! This was no accident. Oh, you wicked, wicked boy," screamed Emma, who could hardly believe the devastation of her beautiful dream room. The ugly writing on the wall, the dripping black paint on her dressing table and floor and the broken chair were enough to break her heart.

"You are a stupid, dangerous and terrible doll," continued Emma. "Wait until Mother and Father see this! They will get rid of you so fast you won't know what happened!"

By now Mary, Mrs Darling and Mr Darling had dashed up the stairs to join them and all the children had clustered outside the room and were peeping in.

"Oh my goodness," Mrs Darling gasped. She looked at her husband with horror.

"Please take Emma away," he said to her. "Mary, I'll need your help to clean this up. Children, we'll talk about this later. Off to the nursery with you now. And Revely, please wait for me, alone, in your room."

Mrs Darling took Emma's arm. "Come along. You can do no good here," she said gently.

"Oh, but everything is ruined. He ruined it. He and Amanda Miranda, they ruin everything or break things or are careless. They are wicked and dangerous. I knew they shouldn't be part of our family," Emma sobbed loudly.

"Emma, you will mind your tongue," said Mrs Darling sharply. She took Emma by the arm and led her past the other children downstairs to the drawing room.

Mr Darling and Mary began the cleaning up. Dolls must never make any changes that people can see, and now there was all this ruin. If the American Lady saw it, heaven knows what would happen.

Mary got clean rags, a mop and a bucket of water from the kitchen and then carefully, patiently, they sponged off most of the paint, which luckily was water paint, not oil paint, and still wet. The carpet still had a small dark spot on it, but it didn't show too much in the flowered pattern.

But the lovely, graceful chair was a problem. The leg was broken off cleanly, snapped the way you can snap a wooden matchstick, and it was about the same size. Mr Darling fetched some glue and a pin and a hammer. Carefully, he put the pin through the chair seat and into the top of the broken leg and began hammering away until the pin disappeared through the seat and into the leg, attaching it once again. It was a clever job, and the leg was stronger than ever because it was reinforced with the steel of the pin.

Revely, meanwhile, went upstairs with the others, and left them at the nursery to go into his room. All the little dolls were too shocked to talk to him.

"I don't care," said Revely to himself, but he did. He sat down at the edge of the bed, and felt afraid. And then his idea of a tightrope on the roof came to him again. "I'll go and do that," he thought to himself. "I'll show everyone that I don't care." In just a moment he was out of the window with the same string he had used to rescue Boots.

Amanda Miranda sat with the other dolls in the nursery. She felt awful. She wanted everyone to love one another, and now this had happened. Would the Darlings hate them now? And poor Revely. Why did he have to do it?

"Bayruth thinks it was an accident," said Johnsley.

"Oh, don't be silly. You can accidentally *spill* paint but you can't accidentally *write* on the wall," said Enid.

"Bayruth says you can. And he says that Revely is very sorry and won't be bad again."

"Oh be quiet, Johnsley. Bayruth is wrong and

anyway he isn't even real."

"Think what you want, but I know the truth," said Johnsley in an offended voice. "Bayruth thinks you're rude."

At that moment the three of them, and perhaps Bayruth, heard a scribble scrabble noise on the roof. It sounded like branches scratching, but much heavier.

"What's that?" asked Enid, frightened.

"Bayruth thinks it's a monster," said Johnsley.

"Oh, no," gasped Amanda Miranda, and ran to the window. By hanging out of it she could just see Revely's feet, inching up the slates of the roof. Her dream came back to her, and for a moment she almost believed she could see him sliding off, whirling into space. She felt sick and dizzy.

"Revely, you come down at once," she whispered. "You are already in enough trouble."

"I don't care," he retorted. "I'm going to walk this tightrope and then run away to the Barzinis and become a circus doll."

"Don't be silly. You are a million miles away from them and anyway, you are made of china. If you fall, you'll smash. Come down at once."

"Bayruth definitely thinks you should come down," added Johnsley. "Please, please do."

"I don't care," repeated Revely. "I won't." And to prove it he scrambled further up the roof towards the chimney.

"Let's get Mother," suggested Enid.

"No, wait," Amanda Miranda insisted. She felt Revely was already in enough trouble and she could fix this. But oh, her dream terror was so strong, so very strong that she felt she might faint. Yet she had to save Revely. So, carefully, one foot at a time, Amanda Miranda climbed out of the window and onto the ledge under it, slowly, slowly moving towards Revely on the roof.

"Revely, come down now," she hissed. "Don't make things worse than they already are."

Revely turned and saw his sister balanced on the edge. "What are you doing?" he almost yelled. "Go back, get off the roof."

"You get off the roof and I will."

"Don't be stupid. I know how to do this. You don't."

"Revely, come in or I'm going to bring you in."

"Bayruth really thinks you should both come in,"

shouted Johnsley from the window. He was squeezing his eyes tightly shut.

"I'm getting Mother," said Enid. Revely paused for a moment. He was afraid for Amanda Miranda, and then, all in a wave he was afraid for himself. The roof was high and the floor so very far below. Hesitantly, he began climbing down the slanted slates.

"Hurry up," said Amanda Miranda, taking a breath in relief. "And be careful."

Slowly Revely took down the string and worked his way down the roof to his sister. Together they stepped towards the window. Just at that moment, Amanda Miranda slipped. Revely reached out and steadied her, pushing her towards the window, but he lost his balance, and in a flash he fell backwards.

"Oh, oh no," cried Amanda Miranda. And she turned her head in time to see him sailing off the edge, into space, a horrified look on his face. "Revely," she screamed, as he plummeted down, down to the cruel, hard floor below. Then all was silent, except for the sound of Johnsley running away from the window.

It took Amanda Miranda a few very difficult moments to get the courage to pull herself to the edge and look. She could only bear to look for a moment, but in that moment she saw Revely's leg sheared off as cleanly as the chair leg he had broken in Emma's room. It was flung far from his body. She closed her eyes before she could see any more pieces.

"Revely," she whispered. But there was no response.

The next thing Amanda Miranda remembered was being gathered into Mr Darling's arms and carried to Revely's bed, where Mrs Darling tucked her in. She could hear the sounds of the household – Enid whispering in the hall and Johnsley crying and repeating over and over, "Bayruth told them not to." And then she didn't remember any more.

Dolls can Pretend, but there are limits to Pretending, and this was one. They could not Pretend that Revely did not fall, they could not Pretend he was fine. And they could not fetch him up in pieces from the floor since the string had fallen with him.

Mary took the children to the kitchen, Mrs Darling sat with the silent Amanda Miranda and Mr Darling went alone to the darkened library.

The door opened and Emma burst into the dim room. "Oh, Father!" she cried. "It's all my fault."

Mr Darling turned to her kindly. "Of course it isn't, Emma. It was an accident, a terrible accident, but you are not to blame."

"But I am," cried Emma.

"Emma, you were nowhere near the roof."

"You don't understand. I was jealous of Amanda Miranda and spiteful and mean. I made her and Revely feel left out. I wanted them to be left out. It made me feel better about myself, somehow."

"Why don't you tell me about it," Mr Darling said kindly. His voice was always deep and soft, but to poor unhappy Emma it sounded now as deep and as comforting as a feather bed. So she told about how she hadn't wanted to share: not her parents, not her room, not anything.

"I thought I was never going to have anything that was mine, that I cared about, that was only for me. And so, I didn't want Amanda Miranda to have anything either. Father, I was so unkind! And I provoked Revely. He behaved badly because of me.

He isn't a bad doll, Father. It's all my fault. And I'm so ashamed."

"My poor dear girl," responded Mr Darling, taking her hand. "You have been so very unhappy and I had no idea. If your life feels empty, of course it is difficult to share and give to others. Empty jugs cannot pour. Ah, we all badly need a child of our own." He sighed. "I had no idea," he repeated sadly. "Can you forgive yourself?" he asked Emma.

"But that's the worst of it," cried Emma. "I had been feeling so much better since we moved into the house. I have my room and those wonderful flowers and my photography. I'd begun to like my life. And then when I saw what Revely had done I felt so angry, as if he had ruined everything. But it was I, I who ruined everything! And now Revely is shattered and Amanda Miranda is done in and none of us can ever be happy again."

"Emma, Emma, my dear, remember that each of us has his own needs and you do not control everything. Revely did misbehave, and that was his choice. You were unkind, or at least very angry, but you didn't put Revely out onto that roof and you didn't want him or Amanda Miranda to come to any harm."

"Oh, of course I didn't," she burst out. "I would give anything to have been able to stop them. I wish it were I instead of he who fell. It should have been I. And I love them so much. I didn't know how much until now." Emma hung her head. "Oh, Father," she whispered. "You must be so disappointed in me."

"I could never be disappointed in you Emma. You are a very good doll and I love you." Emma would remember those words for ever.

"Oh, Father, do you think Revely might be mendable? Is he shattered beyond repair?"

"We don't know, my dear. Only Amanda Miranda saw and she isn't speaking just now. The American Lady may help. We can only hope."

11
Aftermath

Amanda Miranda was not speaking. She lay for hours on Revely's bed, staring at the ceiling. Sometimes the children peeped in, but she would not speak. Mary or Mrs Darling sat at the foot of the bed, keeping silent vigil.

Time passed very slowly for all the dolls. Since most dolls cannot cry, it is especially difficult for them to be sad. Imagine, if you can, something awful happening to you and knowing that you would never be able to cry about it, and you may feel a little of what the Darlings felt.

"I feel as if I will crack in pieces," said Enid as she stood with Johnsley, staring out of the bedroom window.

"Don't crack into pieces," he whispered. "Don't even say those words."

"I know it's hard out here in the Real, but this is too hard," said Mary. When she wasn't with Amanda Miranda, she sat alone in the kitchen, with Buster on her lap. "I can't remember feeling so sad that I couldn't even work. T'isn't right. T'isn't right. That poor little thing."

Emma comforted Eugenia, who didn't know exactly

what was wrong. She held Eugenia and played with her quietly, though it was very wearing on Emma to smile and play. Somehow, she felt doing something difficult was the best thing for her just then.

Mr and Mrs Darling sat together in the drawing room. Neither spoke, but the silence between them was the comforting kind when both dolls knew what the other was feeling.

"I'm grateful you are here, Armstead," Mrs Darling said at length. "I blame myself. I saw trouble coming with Emma, and I knew how Revely could be provoking. I should have spoken to them. And Amanda Miranda, she always is too willing to take the blame and sacrifice herself. Oh, Armstead, I should have known."

"You cannot control and fix everything, my dear. We must simply wait," said Mr Darling.

It was, of course, very terrible for Amanda Miranda. She wouldn't talk at all – she just lay on the brass bed in Revely's room and stared at the sloping ceiling of the attic. Just like Emma and Mrs Darling, she felt responsible for the accident and was flooded with guilt and remorse. Over and over again she saw the image of Revely hurling out into space, falling and twisting all the way down, and she saw what happened when he hit the floor. Amanda Miranda played it over and over in her head like a monster movie projector that goes over the same film a thousand times. It made her feel sick in her stomach, and so unhappy that she felt she could not bear it.

Now this part of the story I'm going to tell quickly because I know it feels bad not to know what happens. Authors call this "suspense" and say that it is necessary for good stories, but to me it just feels like worry.

The American Lady came home at last and was very upset to find Revely lying on the floor. She said "Oh, no!" and scooped the pieces up carefully. "How could this have happened?" she wondered aloud and hurried from the room. She didn't come back for a long time.

It was the next morning when she returned. She opened the doll's house.

"I have taken Revely to the doll hospital," she said. "He is damaged but they think they can mend him. It will take several weeks. Let's have no more accidents." Then she said something very curious. "It has upset the schedule, but it may work out all for the best."

None of the Darlings thought about the schedule and what it might mean. Perhaps it was just as well.

The days passed very slowly, but on Friday Tally came in and lifted Amanda Miranda from her bed.

"I am going to the doll hospital and Amanda Miranda is coming with me," she announced. In a moment she was gone before the Darlings even had a chance to say goodbye. As Amanda Miranda wasn't speaking, it made little difference.

"Why is she taking Amanda Miranda?" asked Enid.

"Oh, Mother, is it all right?" asked Emma.

"We will have to hope so," Mrs Darling said, and turned to Mr Darling. "Could she be separating both of them from us? Is Revely shattered and she is getting rid of them both?" She whispered so that the children couldn't hear. "Oh, Armstead, what do you think?"

"We will hope and I think it will be all right. There is nothing we can do."

"Bayruth says it's fine," said Johnsley. "They are just going to buy new clothes."

"Oh, don't be silly. Bayruth is the stupidest bear and he isn't even real," snapped Enid. Johnsley, and probably Bayruth too, were silent.

If waiting had been hard before, this day was the hardest. It was past tea time when Tally returned and put on the light in the dining room.

"Well, here we are," she said, and took out a parcel. It seemed to the Darlings that it took her hours to untie the string and open the box, although she really was as quick as she could be. At last she finished, and, one at a time, took out Revely and Amanda Miranda.

But what a difference! Instead of the lumpy grey velvet, the two of them wore jaunty new sailor suits.

Revely had gold buttons on his coat, and crisp short trousers. He stood up perfectly straight and sound, although round his leg, under his trousers, was a neat white bandage, all tied up ship-shape. Amanda Miranda had a middy collar, a red sailor's knot, and a crisply pleated skirt. She looked wonderful, and so did Revely. And the clothes were beautifully made, sewn not glued.

"Oh, my darlings," cried their mother. "I'm so happy you are home!"

Tally put them all together in the drawing room. "Perhaps you would like to be alone," she said, and left them.

"Are you all right?" asked Mrs Darling, hugging them both.

"Did it hurt?" asked Johnsley.

"You look beautiful," said Enid.

"Can you forgive me?" asked Emma.

"Yes, yes, thank you, and yes," answered Amanda Miranda and Revely. And everyone hugged.

"We are so happy you are home," said Mr Darling.

"See, Bayruth knew that they were getting new clothes," said Johnsley. Enid looked at him hard.

"What was the hospital like? How do you feel? We missed you terribly. We were very worried. Are you all right? What did they do to you? And who made you the clothes?" Question followed question followed question.

So Revely explained how after the fall he was taken to the doll hospital where a kind gentleman put a pin in his leg, just the way Mr Darling had fixed the chair.

"There is a line that shows, so he covered it with

the bandage," Revely told them. "I also have a chip but my hair cushioned the fall, so other than that, I'm as good as new. It is lucky my hair is so thick, isn't it?"

Revely went on: "There was also a lady there who measured me carefully. They had to cut off my old clothes, so she sewed these for me. And Tally-Ho told her about Amanda Miranda, and she made up a sailor suit for her too, since her measurements are the same. Tally said it had to be done by today because of her schedule, and the lady worked for hours and hours into the night. Isn't it a grand surprise?"

And everyone agreed that it was, and they all talked it over, and Emma tried to tell Amanda Miranda and Revely how sorry she was and Revely told Mr and Mrs Darling how he would stop being so careless, and there were more hugs before bedtime. And then Emma turned to her sister.

"Amanda Miranda, would you like me to teach you photography?" Emma asked. "I have all of the things up in our room to show you."

"It's so good to be home isn't it Amanda Miranda?" Revely sighed.

"Mother called us Darlings" was all Amanda Miranda said, but it was enough.

And now you probably think this is the happy ending. But if you've been looking at this book carefully, you'll know there are more pages and the story isn't finished at all. Because just a day after Amanda Miranda and Revely came home, the American Lady came into the dining-room and took the whole family out of their house. She set them back on the dining-room table, and began emptying their house of furniture. Then the porter and two other big men picked up their wonderful home and put it back into the crate that it had come in, while the American Lady supervised. Then she turned to the table and, one by one, all of their furniture, dishes, pictures and other things were also packed away.

"Oh, what is happening?" asked Mrs Darling. But, of course, none of the dolls knew the answer. They just huddled together on the vast table top and could only wait.

"It's happened at last," Mrs Darling cried. "We are being collected!"

When everything was packed and the house was gone, the American Lady picked up the dolls, one by one, and put them back into the box they had been shipped in, wrapping them carefully in tissue paper just as before. I truly hope that you don't hate the American lady, and you will know why later.

"Perhaps we are being sent to some children," Mr Darling hoped.

"Oh, Mother, my room, my flowers!" cried Emma.

"Bayruth says this is a vacation," said Johnsley.

"We are being sent to the seaside."

"You don't send a whole house away on vacation," snapped Enid.

"This time we do," answered Johnsley.

The journey in the box this time was very different from the first. The dolls were frightened and had little hope. For a while Enid wondered if perhaps Bayruth was right as he had been right about the new clothes for Amanda Miranda and Revely, but the rest of the dolls were grim.

And it appeared that this time Bayruth was decidedly wrong, for after only a few hours the dolls were unpacked and they found themselves back in a toyshop.

12
Almost the End

"Why, this is where we bought our furniture," said Mrs Darling.

The family were all taken to the big front window and there was their house waiting for them.

"Oh, Mother, it's all right. There's the house. We'll be fine now," smiled Amanda Miranda, relieved.

"Oh no, Armstead," cried Mrs Darling. "We are going to become a Display!" And though the children didn't know what that meant, the despair in their mother's voice told them it was not a good thing at all. To Amanda Miranda it sounded like a knick-knack and, of course, she was right.

It was the American Lady who unpacked them and she had many people to help her. Mr Darling listened carefully and it became clear to him that she worked for this great toyshop. She was very pleased because she had finished the doll's house in time for it to be on display in the shop. Everyone in the shop was being very kind and excited.

"Oh, Miss Rendal, you've outdone yourself."

"Splendid job, Miss Rendal."

She was obviously important in the shop, but to the

Darlings at that moment she was worse than a Serious Collector.

The next weeks were truly terrible for the Darlings. Day after day, people came and stared at them and their wonderful doll's house. And while the Darlings liked people and enjoyed their admiration, Mr and Mrs Darling knew that they were all in great danger. For to be left as a Display was as bad as being without a child to love and be loved by.

"We will have no life," Mrs Darling repeated over and over to herself. "We shall never be loved." She was in the drawing room with Eugenia, who was crawling on the hearth rug, and at last her courage failed her. She felt no hope and that is when dangerous despair takes over. But, "Be brave," she said to her family.

"We are, we are," said Amanda Miranda who was sitting in the library with her father, reading.

"You heard your mother," chided Mary, who was hanging laundry in the kitchen, assisted by Enid.

"We are being brave," answered Revely, who was playing Noah's Ark with Johnsley on the stairs.

"So is Bayruth," added Johnsley.

But the days and the weeks stretched out. There was no privacy for the dolls. They could never move at all. Imagine how you would feel if you had to play statue for even one hour. The Darlings were frozen. Faces stared in at them. They were pleased to entertain the children and looked yearningly at them through the glass, but they needed to be held and played with, not just looked at. It made the pain worse, to be so close to all that attention, and yet not to have a child of their own.

The crowds came from early in the morning through the whole day and even into the night.

"Look at the tiny clothes pegs!"

"See the alarm clock on the bedside table!"

"Oh, isn't the crate of apples just perfect!"

"That conservatory is beautiful! I wish I had a greenhouse like that!"

"Oh, I wish I had a doll's house like that."

But beside the doll's house, on a neatly lettered sign were the words, "Doll's house for display only. Not for sale."

"We are a Display," thought Mrs Darling over and over again. "We will never know a child's love." She wept.

When things are very bleak it is most difficult to have hope and it was a very bleak time for the dolls. Often, they were angry; sometimes they were frightened.

"But we love each other and we must be brave," urged Mr Darling.

Late at night, Amanda Miranda would look out of the library window and watch the snow fall on the Real. It was pretty but she felt so sad. After finding a home and a family at last, the idea of languishing on as a Display, with no more tea time, no more fun, no more chores, no more life, was almost too sad for her to bear.

It was holiday time and the shop was even more crowded with children. And still the Darlings sat in the window, day after day.

New Year's Eve came and the dolls could hear the assistants in the shop behind them wish each other a Happy New Year. The Darlings felt sadder and more frightened than ever. The New Year did not look promising for them.

"We must keep hoping," said Mrs Darling, but she was close to despair.

And then, on New Year's Day morning, when the streets were quiet and few people were about, the American Lady appeared at the window. With her were a little girl and boy who gazed as she pointed

105

out the dolls to them. The children were excited.

"Oh, may we go inside, Aunty?" the dolls could hear the little girl ask.

Now most shops are closed on New Year's Day, but the American Lady had a special set of keys because she worked at the toyshop and was trusted. In just a few moments, she and the children were in the window, and the doll's house was turned round.

The American Lady reached inside. "Rachel, Michael, I'd like you to meet the Darlings. Mr and Mrs Darling, allow me to introduce my niece Rachel and my nephew Michael."

"Oh, Aunty Justine," are they really for us?" asked Rachel, her eyes glowing with love.

"Indeed they are."

"I want to play with you," said Michael, lifting Revely up. "I think we could have fun."

"I bet you will," laughed the American Lady. "He's the very mischief."

"Oh, Aunty Justine, they are so wonderful! I love them all," exclaimed Rachel.

"I hoped you would," answered the American Lady, who, in case you haven't guessed yet, is me. If you don't believe it, just look at my name on the cover of this book.

"How will we get the house home?" asked Michael. "Can we take it on the train to Massachusetts?"

"It will have to be packed and shipped, and we will do it next week. Can you wait that long? I still must take some pictures."

"Oh, it will be so hard! But just knowing that they are on their way home to us is so wonderful, I can wait," said Rachel.

"I can't," said Michael. "Please may we play with them now?"

So that is how it happened that on New Year's morning in a big toy shop, the Darlings were played with for the first time.

I'm certain I don't have to describe to you what playing is like. Rachel Pretended for Mrs Darling, Mary, Emma, Enid and, of course, for Amanda Miranda. Michael (who is two years younger) Pretended for Johnsley, Revely and, for Eugenia too. And both of them Pretended for Mr Darling. And perhaps because the Darlings had waited so long or perhaps because Rachel and Michael were very good at it, the playing and Pretending were perfect.

"Let's pretend that it's just before the holidays and everyone is getting ready," said Rachael.

"Yes, let's," responded Amanda Miranda.

"Oh yes," said Emma.

"I think Mrs Darling is secretly wrapping presents in her bedroom."

"Yes, I am!" cried Mrs Darling.

"And Mr Darling has brought in a parcel. It's supposed to be a surprise but Johnsley and Enid are peeping," Rachel said.

"Yes, we are," they shouted.

"Emma is taking a secret snapshot of the presents."

"Oh, I'd love to!" she exclaimed.

"I think Mary has the turkey already in the oven. Now she is making holiday buns, but she's run out of sugar."

"How could that have happened?" asked Mary.

"Because Revely has taken the sugar bag up to his room to feed a mouse," added Michael.

"Oh, no!" cried Mary.

"Oh, yes!" cried Revely.

"And Amanda Miranda is in the hall with Boots, who is after the mouse. He's a very good kitten," said Rachel.

"Oh," breathed Amanda Miranda, "this is better than I ever imagined." And it was.

At last, though it was hard, the children had to leave. "But you'll be with us soon," they assured the Darlings and themselves.

"Aunty, may I leave my other present here?" asked Michael.

"Of course," I said. "I'll send it with the rest."

Out of his pocket, Michael pulled a perfect miniature teddy bear. "I shall have Mr Darling give it to Johnsley."

Then Johnsley was lifted into the drawing room to join his mother and father. There, on Mr Darling's lap, sat the teddy bear.

"Hello, Bayruth," said Johnsley. "What are you

doing here?" he asked calmly. "Come up on the stairs, I was waiting for you. I wanted to tell you that we have a child of our own. Well, we have two childs."

Mrs Darling smiled, and for once did not correct his grammar. "You're right. We have two childs of our own," she said, and all the Darlings laughed.

13
The End for Now

The Darlings had wonderful times with Michael and Rachel in Boston. And as they were both careful children, they took good care of their dolls.

"It's all come out so well because of the children," said Amanda Miranda.

"No, it was Bayruth," said Johnsley.

"No, it's the American Lady," said Enid and Emma together.

"We was lucky," said Revely.

"We *were* lucky," corrected Mrs Darling, "And brave."

"We didn't lose hope," said Mr Darling. Mary nodded wisely.

Of course, whenever I came up to visit, I brought a surprise for them from the toy store. That is how Revely got his bicycle, how the flower garden was started, and how Amanda Miranda got a playhouse.

I hope you won't be angry to learn that once a year I did borrow the house back for the window display, but I know for a fact, that Rachel and Michael didn't mind, since they came down for a visit. It made them proud! And I know that the Darlings didn't mind. They even came to look upon it as an exciting adventure – as long as it was only temporary.

The reason I know it is because last Christmas, which was years after the first one, Amanda Miranda told Rachel the whole story, and Rachel told me so I could write it down. And now I have. It's taken me a long time, and I'm quite tired, so I'm going to stop now.